PASSAGE TO PETROGRAD

Russia, 1924. Lenin is dying. Soviet Russia is on the brink of an explosion...

King George V decides he must help his one key relative in Russia to escape. In 1918 he had refused asylum to his cousin the Tsar – now the King orders that Serge, the Tsar's illegitimate son, be saved. 'C', the head of the British Secret Service, gives the task to Common Smith VC and the crew of the *Swordfish*, but 'C' is playing a double game. He sees Serge as a future Tsar – little does he know he is not the only one who doesn't want Serge to reach Britain.

PASSAGE TO PETROGRAD

PASSAGE TO PETROGRAD

by

Charles Whiting

Magna Large Print Books
Long Preston, North Yorkshire,
BD23 4ND, England.

British Library Cataloguing in Publication Data.

Whiting, Charles
    Passage to Petrograd.

    A catalogue record of this book is
    available from the British Library

    ISBN   978-0-7505-2809-2

First published in Great Britain in 1995
by Severn House Publishers Limited

Copyright © 1995 by Charles Whiting

Cover illustration © Keith Page by arrangement with
Temple Rogers

Magna Large Print is an imprint of Library Magna Books Ltd.

Printed and bound in Great Britain by
T.J. (International) Ltd., Cornwall, PL28 8RW

Author's Note

In the third decade of this century, Captain Sir de Vere Smith, VC, DSO (and bar), OBE (mil. div.) carried out some very strange and important missions for the 'King-Emperor', as the old man called George V. If it had succeeded, Common Smith VC might well have changed the history of the world. The evil empire of Communism might have collapsed fifty years before Gorbachev. World War II might well not have been fought. Unfortunately, Common Smith's bold attempt to alter the course of world history failed.

Now at last, thanks to the 'seventy year rule', the Public Record Office at Kew has been allowed to release the details of what Common Smith VC and his brave crew of the *Swordfish* actually did in the January of 1924. *Passage to Petrograd* tells the story of those brave young men so long ago. It is not a pretty story. It is one of treachery, murder,

and lust. But in those days there were no pretty stories...
C. W. York, 1995

SAVAGE PRELUDE

The killers came just after midnight.

The old woman knew they would. She had lain awake most of that hot July night, listening to the guards outside, drinking and swearing and boasting of their prowess with the local whores. She had half guessed all this was leading up to savage murder.

Now as the trucks, which had brought the killers, braked to a stop outside, she rose from her bed, fully dressed save for her boots. She tugged them on swiftly. Silently she walked over to where the boy slept. She placed her hand over his sweet mouth to stop him crying out and whispered into his ear. 'Serge, get up. At once. They're here.'

The little boy, with the startling blue eyes of his father, rose immediately. He, too, was fully dressed. She slipped on his shoes. On tiptoe they went down the dark stairs. Outside, an ominous silence had fallen, as if the guards had suddenly realised, drunk as they were, that what was soon to happen would mean the end of an era. But the killers were still there, the old woman knew that all right. Through the windows of the house which had been whitewashed as soon as they had been imprisoned here, she could see their dark shapes outlined by the trucks' headlights. Perhaps they were smoking or more probably drinking, she told herself, giving themselves courage for the dastardly deed soon to come.

'Is it them, *Babuska?*' Serge whispered.

'*Da,*' she hissed. She crossed herself and then opened the door of the big wall cupboard which led to their hiding place. It had been the 'Little Fathers'' idea. Two days before, he had come to her while the others were having their afternoon nap, as was their custom even in captivity. 'Elena Feodorovna,' he had said a little sadly after she had kissed his hand and risen from her knees, 'I am afraid that we will not survive. Now my cousin will not let us go to England, the Reds will slaughter us in due course.'

She had attempted to protest, but he had silenced her and said, 'The Tsarevich is dying already – poor boy. But one male child must survive. You will ensure that he does.'

'Serge, Your Majesty?' she had asked.

'Yes, he is of good, healthy stock. He is my son and has not inherited the – er – tainted blood of the Tsarina. So let us plan how you will escape.' Together that afternoon they had moved the heavy cupboard in front of the door to the little closet room. When they had finished, he had said to her, 'Elena Feodorovna, wait till the business is finished and they are all gone. Then try to reach safety, though God knows where that is today in my poor accursed Russia. Use these.' And he had handed her a leather wash bag filled with uncut gems.

Now with the gems concealed beneath her underskirt, she ushered the little boy through the wall cupboard and into the dark little room, bare save for two stools and the bucket which she had placed there for emergencies.

Outside there was sudden movement. She placed her mouth close to Serge's left ear. 'They are coming. No noise whatsoever. It doesn't matter what you hear or see. *Pomeya?*'

'*Da, da Babuska!*' Serge whispered obediently.

Suddenly, startlingly, the front door was wrenched open. There was the sound of heavy boots in the hall. Someone said harshly, 'The royal bitches are upstairs, lads.'

'I hope they're naked,' a coarse voice chuckled. 'I don't like to waste time with my bitches.'

13

'None of that,' a harsh voice commanded. 'You know why we're here. *Davoi.*'

The old woman pressed the boy's head into her apron, covering his ears. Now it was going to happen, she knew that. She didn't want her beloved little prince to suffer more than necessary. She held her breath as she heard their boots pass the cupboard in the corridor.

Minutes passed in tense expectation.

Suddenly there was a scream: a woman's scream, high-pitched and hysterical. 'No,' the woman shrieked. 'Please … please … not that… *Please!*'

The old woman bit her bottom lip till the blood came. At her lap, the little boy started to wimper.

Now the night turned into a nightmare. Shots broke out. Someone started to cry in absolute agony. The old woman was sure it was the Tsarevich. Even the slightest blow and the sick boy would bleed to death if the flow wasn't stopped immediately. The old woman began to pray.

Heavy boots clattered down the steps from above. A drunken voice proclaimed loudly, 'I can die a happy man… I've had the Empress… *I've had her!*' The rapist ran outside.

14

Now the firing had stopped. But the screams and shrieks continued. A woman came staggering down the stairs, moaning, 'No more … no more! I can't stand any more.'

The old woman risked a peep through the chink in the cupboard. It was Tatiana, Grand Duchess Tatiana Nicolaevna. She was totally naked, savage blue marks on both her plump breasts, with blood trickling down the inside of her legs. Like a blind person she reeled down the stairs, sobbing hysterically, feeling her way with one hand. Behind her came a pockmarked giant, his flies open, an evil grin on his scarred face. He lunged forward. He caught the Grand Duchess in the small of her back. She stumbled and fell full length in the hall below. The giant whooped in drunken triumph. Next instant he had fastened his dirty hands on her naked back and was pumping away frantically, the sweat streaming down his pockmarked face, while Tatiana Nicolaevna screamed and screamed and screamed…

Five minutes later they brought down the Tsarina. She was naked, too. Her hair was tousled and dishevelled. Already a dark green bruise was beginning to appear on the right side of her noble face. The old woman thought she, too had been raped by the killers. Still she bore herself with dignity. Her face revealed no emotion as she stared back at the killers, who jeered and made obscene threats, while others fumbled with their revolvers.

Then the pockmarked one who had raped the Tsarina's daughter, now lying unconscious and bleeding on the floor, her legs spread in obscene invitation, snarled, 'That's enough. Let's get it over with.' He raised his big revolver. 'Here you are, you royal bitch. Try this one on for size!' He pressed the trigger. The revolver exploded. Scarlet flame stabbed the gloom of the hallway. As if by magic, a bright red hole appeared in the Tsarina's plump right breast. She screamed but didn't go down. The pockmarked killer lowered his aim. He fired again. The second bullet slammed into her stomach just above the patch of black public hair. 'Now you've got a second hole!' he cried, as the Tsarina gave one last scream and sank to the ground, dying.

That second shot seemed to act as a signal for the killers. A couple started to thrust their bayonets into the writhing, twisting body of the Grand Duchess, sticking them into the dying girl in animal frenzy until she lay dead and they were gasping wildly with the effort.

From above came the voice of the Tsar. The old woman could hear it all too clearly. 'Please don't shoot,' he said. 'Pl–' His words were drowned by a burst of firing and he spoke no more.

For what seemed an age to the woman hiding in the cupboard, the firing went on. Then the shots petered away and she could hear the killers running up and down the stairs, smashing china and glasses, overturning furniture in their greedy search for loot, some of them yelling out in triumph when they found something of value, while others cried angrily, 'Hey, you greedy swine, I saw that first!'

In the end they finished looting. Outside, the engines of the trucks started up and the old woman guessed they would take away the bodies of the murdered royal family. She was right. Two of the killers came staggering down the stairs, bearing the dead body of the Tsar, the blood dripping from it as they did so. Hurriedly the old woman crossed herself as the corpse passed.

The Tsarevich followed. His frail, dead body was cradled in the arms of a big, one-eyed rogue of a fellow, so that he looked as if he might only be asleep. The old woman felt the tears well up in her eyes at the sight. Then came the women, dragged carelessly down the hall by their hands, their heads bumping up and down, lolling from side to side cruelly.

The door crashed shut. Someone shouted to the guards on the perimeter fence, 'All right, you men, you can go off to your homes now! They're all dead. You won't be needed any longer!'

'Yes, comrades,' the guards shouted back. 'Thank you. You've ridden us of the royal swine at last!'

The first truck started to move away. A few moments later it was followed by the second. There was the sound of the men's boots on the road outside which led to Ekaterinburg. Slowly the night silence fell over that house of death. Carefully, very carefully, the old woman released the boy from her grip. 'I think the bad men have all gone,' she warned him in a taut whisper. 'But don't say anything. I shall have a look.'

Heart beating like a triphammer, she opened the door. Her hand shot to her mouth. With a sheer effort of will she stopped herself from crying out. There was blood everywhere. On the floor, on the bullet-marked walls. A woman's patent leather shoe lay on the stairs. The cuddly dog toy which the little Tsarevich always took to bed with him sat next to it. *'Boshe moi … boshe moi,'* she whispered to herself and reeled with shock. Still she forced herself to go on, stepping over the pools of blood and heaps of broken glass.

Cautiously she peered out of the door.

In the yellow light cast by the summer moon, she could see that the perimeter fence, which had been manned by Red Guards day and night ever since they had been brought to this prison, was deserted. Far off down the road, which led to the town, there were half a dozen dark figures. They were guards. Otherwise nothing.

Using the last of her strength, she went inside and picked up the boy, holding his face pressed tight to her ample bosom so that he could not see the blood and devastation. Outside she put him down once more and leaned against the wall to recover.

Serge looked at her solemnly. For a little boy of six he was strangely composed. The screams, the shouts, the shots seemed to have had little effect upon him. Quite calmly, he asked, 'What now, *Babuska?*'

The old woman licked her dry lips.

19

Suddenly she was overcome by the great responsibility that had been thrust upon her this night. 'Serge Nicholai,' she choked, 'you will come with me to my village. There you will be safe.'

'When will that be, *Babuska?*' he asked solemnly, looking at her with those piercing blue eyes of his.

'I don't know.' Her voice broke for a moment, then she continued, 'But you must be saved for Russia.'

'Why?'

'Because you are now the last of the Romanovs.' Then without another word she took his hand and they set off, a little boy and a bent old woman. Minutes later the yellow night had swallowed them up...

BOOK ONE

THE WAY IN

Chapter One

Lieutenant de Vere Smith, VC shivered. He dug his head deeper into the warm serge of his greatcoat. Next to him, his second-in-command, 'Dickie' Bird, said, 'Oh my sainted aunt, heaven help a sailor on a night like this.'

'Keep it down to a dull roar, Dickie,' Smith said. He peered through the fog, which was coming in over the Irish Sea, wet, cold and miserable. 'The Paddies can't be far off now, you know.'

'I don't know why these IRA gunrunning chappies can't do so at a decent hour,' 'Dickie' Bird complained in that languid fashion he affected. 'At this time of night a chap ought to be curled up around a couple of large pink gins, or even better, an eager and willing lady of the night, what?'

'What.' Despite the tension and strain, Smith smiled to himself. Dickie, who had been at school with him at Harrow and had now been his second-in-command in the *Swordfish* since 1918, never seemed to flap.

But beneath that flippant, languid manner of his, there was a steel-hard purpose and determination. After all, it wasn't every midshipman who had won the DSC at the age of seventeen.

'What's the drill?' Dickie asked after a while as the *Swordfish*, the long, lean, powerful ex-naval torpedo boat, chugged through the grey turgid sea at a snail's pace. 'Do we try to take them alive?'

Smith shook his head firmly. *'No!* We don't want any trouble with the Irish Free State authorities. Sink 'em and run – that's C's orders.'

Dickie nodded his head as if in approval. 'I suppose they deserve it,' he said. 'These awful bog Irish roman candles, always blowing people up or shooting 'em. Deuced bore–'

'Shut up!' Smith hissed urgently. 'I think I can hear something.' He cocked his head to one side. 'Yes. Do you hear it, Dickie?'

Hastily Dickie Bird stubbed out the gold-rimmed cigarette, a special style he had made for him specially at a little shop in Bond Street. 'Yes. It's got to be them.'

Smith didn't hesitate. He turned to Chief Petty Officer 'Sandy' Ferguson, next to him on the torpedo boat's tiny bridge. 'All right,

Chiefie,' he commanded, 'get ready to give me all you've got.'

'Ay ay, sir,' the ancient grizzled CPO, who the crew sneered, 'was so bleeding old, he'd served with Nelson at Trafalgar', answered.

Down on the deck the crew of the *Swordfish* had also heard the steady chug-chug of the other craft. Now all of them stood by their weapons, straining to get a first glimpse of the gunrunner.

'We're sure they'll be heading for Greencastle, Kilkeel, Annalong … one of those small ports below the Mourne Mountains,' C had told Smith at the briefing in that mysterious office of his in Queen Anne's Gate. 'In a couple of hours after landing the arms, the murdering devils can spirit them away into the mountains. It's your job to stop them before they get that far.' He had stared hard at the young ex-naval officer with those penetrating blue eyes of his, which brooked no opposition. 'I know what you will do is illegal and can be classed as cold-blooded murder. But that's the name of the game, Smith. *Sink 'em and kill 'em!*'

Now as the steady throb of the tramp steamer's engines came nearer and nearer, Smith remembered those harsh words in C's office. But he knew it had to be done.

25

There had to be an end to the killing in Ireland. It had been going on now since the Easter Rebellion of 1916. Now eight years later, when everyone had thought with the creation of an Irish Free State it would stop, the blood-letting still continued.

'There she is, sir!' 'Ginger' Kerrigan's voice broke into his grim reverie. 'To port!'

Smith swung round. Out of the swirling wet fog, an ancient tramp steamer came plodding through the water, its single stack belching black coal fumes.

'About four hundred tons' displacement is my guess,' Dickie Bird said. 'So far the bounders haven't spotted us.'

'They soon will,' Smith said grimly and then he leaned out of the bridgehouse and ordered, 'Tubes, stand by with the tin fish!'

'Ay ay, sir,' Tubes, otherwise known as Leading Hand Harp, an experienced torpedo man, who had been loaned to the *Swordfish* for this operation, answered smartly and bent over his long deadly weapon, a steel tube filled with one ton of high explosive.

Slowly, Ferguson, at the wheel, began to close with the gunrunner, cutting steadily through the Irish Sea heading for the coast, its deck completely blacked-out save for one single riding light.

'Not a sausage to be seen,' Dickie said, as they drew even nearer. 'Could well be the jolly old Flying Dutchman.'

Smith didn't answer. His whole attention was concentrated on the ancient tramp steamer. They were still within Irish territorial waters. If 'Tubes' missed and the steamer could make a run for it, they might well bump into the Irish Navy and then, as Dickie always put it, 'the fur and snot' would really begin to fly.

'Three hundred, sir,' CPO Ferguson sang out at the wheel. A moment later, he called, *'Two hundred and fifty sir … two hundred sir….!'*

Smith, his brain racing electrically with excitement, knew it was now or never. 'Tubes,' he called, as the first burst of tracer started to arch its way to the *Swordfish*, gathering speed by the instant, 'fire one!'

Leading Hand Harp didn't hesitate. He pulled the lever. There was a soft plop. A flash of smoke. Suddenly the *Swordfish* shuddered as the torpedo shot from her bows and plunged into the water with a fierce burst of bubbles. Next moment the enemy slugs raked the deck of the little torpedo boat and Tubes yelled out with pain, his right arm riddled with bullets. He slapped to the deck unconscious, or dead, Smith couldn't tell.

27

At the Lewis gun, Ginger Kerrigan took up the challenge. He swung the heavy machine gun round, tucked the butt into his skinny shoulder, and pressed the trigger, crying, 'Here ye are, mate, try this on fer frigging size!' White and red tracer started to hiss towards the tramp steamer like a flight of angry hornets.

Next to Smith a suddenly tense Dickie started to count off the seconds. *'Three ... four ... five...'* He stopped abruptly and stared at Smith, aghast. 'Oh my sainted aunt!' he yelled. 'Poor old Tubes has gorn and missed her!'

'Blast and damn!' Smith yelled above the snap-and-crackle of the fire fight, ignoring the slugs pattering against the bridgehouse like heavy tropical rain on a tin roof. 'And she is turning about!'

Now the tramp steamer, belching smoke as she did so, was turning slowly. Men were lining up, firing as they ran for the upper decks to get a better aim. Cursing furiously, Ginger Kerrigan fired a whole pan of ammunition at them. A man flung up his hands dramatically, clawing the air, as if he were climbing an invisible ladder. Next moment he smacked down on the deck. Kerrigan laughed crazily and yelled, 'Serves yer right, yer Mick git!' He whipped on another pan and started firing again.

But already the gunrunner was disappearing into the fog and now Smith could hear the mournful wail of a fog horn. Obviously they were getting dangerously close to the coast of the Irish Free State. Something had to be done and done quickly, or the vessel would escape. 'Give her full, Chiefie!' he yelled above the racket. 'We'll head her off, Sandy.' Ferguson needed no urging. In that dour Scots manner of his, he hated most nationalities save his Calvinist folk back in Scotland. For him the Irish were 'Papists, fish eaters, who don't even have a pot to piss in'. Now he thrust home the throttles – hard.

The *Swordfish* trembled violently. Smith could feel it vibrating beneath him. Instinctively he grabbed for a stanchion. He knew what was soon to come. The great Thorneycroft engines shrilled and shrieked. They rose to full, ear-splitting power. Her prow rose out of the water immediately. A second later they were hurtling forward at forty knots an hour, trailing a great flying white wake behind them, hitting each fresh wave as if it was a solid brick wall.

In a wild curve, with the radio mast almost touching the surface of the sea, Ferguson flung the *Swordfish* round and raced the craft to the front of the fleeing gunrunner. The Irish tried to meet the challenge. Tracer came racing towards the little torpedo boat like glowing golf balls. Smith ignored the slugs cutting the air everywhere. He dropped from the bridge and, the best he could, with the *Swordfish* slamming into wave after wave, he staggered to where the torpedo rating lay on the deck. He rolled him over. Tubes was dead. Smith cursed, but he knew there was no time for regrets or sorrow now. He had to stop that damned gunrunner.

He dropped to number two tube, and fumbled with the controls. It was a long time since he had worked with torpedoes and he was unfamiliar with the new post-war type used by the Royal Navy. But this, he knew, was the last chance to stop the gunrunner. He found what he needed and, cupping his hands around his mouth, shouted above the tremendous roar of the engines, 'Slow her down, Chiefie!'

Ferguson knew exactly what to do. He brought the boat so that it faced the tramp steamer bow-on, and slowed to half-speed, then to almost dead slow.

Smith licked suddenly dry lips. It was now or never. The gunrunner was five hundred yards away, half shrouded by the wet fog, her shape outlined by the red spurts of machine-gun fire the length of her upper deck. He swallowed hard and hit the lever.

The *Swordfish* shuddered. Plop! The torpedo struck the water. Its electric motor started to run immediately. The bubbles streaked her track. On the bridge, Dickie Bird began to count off the running seconds. On the deck Smith froze, his hands clenched to fists, willing the torpedo to strike home.

Suddenly, startlingly, the old tramp steamer rose out of the water for an instant. Smith could distinctly see her screws churning the air, purposelessly. She slapped back down. Then with a great roar of rending, tearing metal, she began to break up. Like a giant blowtorch, flames seared her deck. Here and there the watchers could see men, outlined a stark black against the angry crimson, writhing and twisting as their bodies were consumed by that terrible flame. A moment later she was going under, the sea around her bubbling and steaming in the intense heat. Then she was gone altogether, leaving behind her a few bits and pieces of debris – a lifebelt, an empty bottle bobbing up and down, a corpse floating face downwards.

Ferguson throttled back altogether. The

Swordfish bobbed up and down silently on the waves. There was no jubilation. The crew had seen enough ships, even enemy ones, go down in their time. It was always something that saddened. On the bridge Dickie saluted. He knew they were gangsters, who had killed innocent women and children, but now they were dead. They deserved a salute, he told himself.

So they stood there for what seemed an age, staring at the ever-increasing circles of water where the gunrunner had gone down in silence, which was only broken when the radio operator came clattering on the deck from below, declaring, 'Skipper, a signal from London. In clear, as well!'

'Read it,' Smith said, hearing his voice coming from what seemed a long way off. He didn't believe in keeping anything from his crew. Under his command, they risked their necks every time they went to sea. They deserved to know what was in store for them. 'Go on, Sparks.'

'From C, sir,' the radio operator said. 'He signals, "Attend me. *HQ. P.D.Q. Bring D.U.s*"'

'Up on the bridge,' Dickie snorted. 'Well, I'll be the doggie's drawers! I know C always wants us in London – *pretty damn quick*. But why the D.U.s – dress uniforms? We ain't going to be presented at Court, are we?' He laughed at his own joke.

But Common Smith VC had no answer to that particular question...

Chapter Two

A little awed, Smith and Bird stood in the Green Drawing Room at Windsor, caps tucked neatly under their right arms. Maids in old-fashioned black dresses were dusting the mirrors which hung everywhere and a flunkey in a white wig and silk breeches was setting the big fire. Everything smelled of camphor and furniture polish, and Smith told himself he had never been in such an overfurnished room since before the War. Obviously nothing had been changed here since the time of Queen Victoria.

Out of the side of his mouth Dickie Bird, obviously a little awed himself, whispered, 'I wonder what the King-Emperor wants with us, old sport? It's all very rum.'

Smith shrugged and said nothing. He didn't know the answer either. The night before, they had arrived at Liverpool Street, where C's representative had met them – a half-colonel with the green brassard of staff intelligence on his right arm. 'The chief says you're to go immediately,' he had said, looking around to see if anyone was listening. 'You've got your glad rags?' He meant their dress uniforms. 'And don't forget the jolly old swords because you're being presented to His Majesty.'

'But what's it all about, sir?' Smith had asked, his handsome face set in a puzzled frown. In reply the intelligence colonel had shaken his head and said, ''Fraid, I can't let on, old boy. It's all very high level and *very* hush-hush, don't you know.'

So now here they were at Windsor Castle, just as puzzled as they had been when they had first received that signal from C, the head of the British Secret Service, two days before.

To the rear of the great room, a door opened and two slim young men sauntered in, dressed in golf suits, the one in front handsome and blond, swinging a golf club as if he was just about to tee off. Immediately the maids and flunkies stopped their work and began bowing and curtseying.

'Beggar me,' Dickie whispered, as he

clicked to attention, 'it's the Prince of Wales and his brother, the Duke of York!'

The Prince of Wales advanced upon them, still swinging his club, as if he were about to send a golf ball flying into space, followed by his brother who kept wringing his hands nervously. 'D'you know who one of these chaps is, Bertie?' the former asked.

'No ... no,' the Duke of York stuttered, wringing his hands even more energetically, 'I ... I ... don't.'

'Common Smith VC.' The Prince stopped his putting and pointed the club at the two young officers. 'Which one?'

Smith, hand on sword, cap under his arm, stepped forward one pace smartly. 'I am, Your Highness,' he snapped, bemused a little that this man would one day be the King-Emperor.

'Hello,' the Prince of Wales said, waving his club. 'Good to see you here. I read about you in the jolly old *Times*. What was it that woman asked you?'

'Whether I was the Honourable de Vere Smythe VC, sir?' Smith answered, feeling himself flush at the memory of the woman reporter who had come into the ward where he was recovering from his wound, dressed as a nurse.

'And you answered, "no, I'm just Common Smith VC. Like Smith's ales from Tadcaster".' The Prince of Wales chortled and laughed. 'Rich, what, Bertie?'

'Yes ... Ed ... Ed ...ward,' his brother stuttered, head twisted to one side, as he forced out the words. 'I ... m ... must say, Smith, I ad ... admire the way you sank that ... Bolshevik ... b ... battleship at Kronstadt in 1918 to win the V ... V ... Victoria Cross.'

'Thank you, sir,' Smith said, flushing even more. Inwardly he cursed the day that reporter had christened him 'Common Smith, VC'. The title had haunted him for six years now.

'They're going to see papa, Bertie,' the Prince of Wales said, swinging his club again. 'We'd better beat it before the big shot comes in, buddy,' he added, assuming an American accent, for the Prince of Wales loved everything American. 'Let's scram.'

'Oh, y ... yes,' his brother stammered, looking fearfully over his skinny shoulder. 'Good ... b ... bye, Common Smith.'

With the Prince of Wales still swinging his club, and his younger brother glancing over his shoulder as if he half expected the Devil himself to enter the drawing room at any moment, they left.

Smith and his old friend Dickie Bird relaxed. Out of the corner of his mouth, Dickie said, 'Rum lot, Smithie, don't y'think?'

Smith gave a little shrug. He was a patriotic young man, intensely loyal to the throne and the Empire. 'Well, Dickie, he *is* the future King-Emperor. I suppose with all that red on the map, all those responsibilities, he has to be a little strange–' He stopped short.

Two flunkies had thrown open the large door at the end of the drawing room. Through it stalked an imposing figure in an immaculate morning suit, who announced, 'His Majesty, the King!'

Again the maids and the flunkies bowed and curtseyed. The large man in the morning suit waved his hand imperiously to the left and right like someone shushing away flies and the servants fled. Next moment a stocky figure with a greying beard entered the room and the two young officers clicked to attention. It was the King-Emperor, George V.

He strode over to them, hands clasped behind his back as if he were back on the quarterdeck of one of the ships he had once commanded in his long career as a regular captain in the Royal Navy. He halted, looked at the two young men hard and then barked, 'Stand at ease ... stand easy!' He sniffed and then the King said, 'Like the cut of your jib. Type of chap who keeps my empire running.' He stared at them, as if he half expected them to say something and when they didn't, he continued with, 'I've talked to C. He says you'd tackle the job – and do it well. I hope so.'

Smith's brain raced suddenly. Obviously C had proposed them for some sort of mission and it had to be important – very important – if it concerned the King-Emperor. He waited tensely for the King's next words.

'Back in '18,' George V went on, 'my cousin the Tsar of All Russia, appealed for my help. As perhaps you know, he and his poor family were imprisoned by those wretched Bolsheviks. Your chief and a few others planned to take them out of their place of imprisonment. A Norwegian engineer called Lied, who was on good terms with the Reds, was to ferry them out on one of his boats to the sawmills of his on the Kara Sea. One of our own craft would rendezvous with them there, race for the Artic and then race for Britain. Got it?' he barked, as if he were back addressing a meeting of his officers in the wardroom.

'Got it, Your Majesty,' they said, as one. Now they could see why the foppish Prince of Wales was scared of his father. Obviously he could be quite frightening.

'Couldn't do it,' the monarch continued. 'Politics, damned politics! Lloyd George said the country was in a funny mood. Said my cousin, the Tsar, was hated by a lot of people in this country. Might tip the balance if he came here in exile. Funny world.' He shook his head, as if he couldn't comprehend life any longer. 'So we left him to his fate. You know what happened then, don't you?' He glared at them.

Again they felt constrained to answer. 'Yes, Your Majesty,' they said as one.

'Yes. Poor Nicky and his family were murdered by those wretches, the Bolos.' Suddenly, surprisingly, there were tears in the King's eyes and Smith realised he wasn't as hard as he appeared. Abruptly he felt sorry for the King, who, with all the responsibilities of the world's greatest empire resting on his aged shoulders, was cursed with such weak sons.

The King sniffed and, tugging a handkerchief out of his sleeve, dabbed his eyes. But when he spoke again, his voice was once more harsh and overbearing. 'Won't happen again, I promise you,' he barked. 'Dammit, this time we'll succeed.'

Smith risked a glance at his companion. He could see the excitement on Dickie's face, as he, too, realised that they were going on a mission for the King-Emperor himself. Ever since 1918, when C had recruited them to help to sink the Red fleet at Kronstadt, where Smith had been wounded and had won the VC, they had undertaken many important missions for the Secret Service, but never one as important as this.

'I know few of the details. C will fill you in on those later. All I know is that the heir to the Romanov throne has been found. He is still in Russia, a mere boy. But he must be rescued before those damned Bolos get their dirty paws on him. Is that understood?'

Again the two of them snapped in unison, 'Yes, Your Majesty.'

'I'm not clear what C has planned for you. But I can tell you this: it will be damned dangerous. C tells me that the Bolos have spies and informers everywhere. All exit ports will be watched. You'll have to be on your toes, the two of you, if you are going to pull it off.' He gave them a wintry smile and nodded to the chamberlain.

The official went across to the fireplace and tugged at the silken rope that hung there. As if he had been waiting there all the time, a flunkey appeared, bearing a silver tray with glasses and bottles and a soda fountain.

'It's a bit early. Sun's not down over the yardarm yet. Still, I don't suppose you'd object to a nip.' He nodded to the flunkey.

Smith looked at Dickie and the other mouthed the words, 'It's only ten in the morning.' Smith nodded his agreement. All the same he accepted the whisky and soda which the flunkey handed him. The King raised his glass of whisky. 'Confusion to our enemies, gentlemen,' he intoned, 'and success to your mission.'

They mumbled something and sipped at their drink, as the King drained his glass in one go. Then to their surprise, he threw the glass at the fireplace where it shattered. The audience was over...

Outside, the tourists were already beginning to gather, cameras at the ready. The Guards were preparing to march off and no one wanted to miss them. 'I say, old bean,' Dickie said, recovered now a little from the strange meeting with the royal princes and the king who threw his glass into the fireplace to end an audience, 'we'd better keep out of the way of those army johnnies when they march off. They look very fierce.'

Smith grinned. They did indeed, he told

himself: all barrel chests, medals and size eleven ammunition boots, polished so much that you could probably see your face in them. 'Right, let's stand to one side, Dickie.'

Twenty yards away, the two men in ankle-length coats and with the un-English hats perched on their cropped heads looked at each other significantly. *'Das sind die, Kurt,'* one of them said in a whisper.

'Bist du sicher?'

'The other man nodded. *'Ganz.'*

'Prima,' the man called Kurt said. He raised his camera, in the same moment that the Guards' band broke into the *British Grenadiers.*

'Parade...' the company commander yelled above the noise of the band, all blaring brass and rattling of the drums, 'will advance ... by the right – *quick march!'*

With the band in the front, the big guardsman swung down the incline leading from the castle, as the crowd of tourists clapped and the cameras clicked.

'Fine sight, eh, Dickie?' Smith said enthusiastically, as the Guards' sergeant major swung by them, pacing stick under his arm, muttering his age-old ritual, 'Come on now, you lot o' pregnant ducks, swing them arms!'

'Best soldiers in the world,' Dickie Bird

agreed. 'Makes you proud to be British.'

'Exactly,' Smith said, as the crowd started to drift away and they could begin to move once more.

Opposite them, the man called Kurt said, *'Dies ist etwas fur den chef. Möchte wissen, was die Beiden vorhaben.'* (The English translation for this sentence is as follows: 'This is something for the chief. I'd like to know what those two are up to.')

Chapter Three

The woman knelt naked in her cheerless hotel room. Fervently she prayed, as she had never prayed before. The ikon to which she prayed was her last remaining possession. But that everything had gone no longer mattered. She finished her prayer and crossed herself in the elaborate Russian fashion. Next door the rusty bedsprings creaked loudly as the whore, who rented the room, serviced yet another from the Red Fleet. She sold her body several times a day for a handful of kopeks or perhaps a couple of cigarettes. They were all like that now, the girl told herself, selling everything they had, including their bodies, in order to survive.

She rose from her knees and took one last look at herself in the flyblown mirror. She thought herself pretty. Her body was thin with hunger but the breasts were still full and firm. She wet her middle finger, listening to the squeaking of the bedsprings and the hectic groans coming from the next room, and ran it gently through her pubes. She gave a little sigh. For years now this had been her only pleasure. She looked at her face in the mirror. It had gone soft and dreamy and a little stupid. She stopped what she was doing immediately, annoyed with herself. 'You've got to be hard with yourself,' she said, talking to herself like lonely people did. 'There is no time for pleasure now – just purpose.' She took one last look at the triangle of jet black hair which had given her so much joy, then turned and began dressing.

Five minutes later she was ready, dressed in the dark grey uniform of the Cheka, the feared Soviet secret police. She crossed to the brass bedstead and put on her belt with the service pistol. That done, she reached under the grubby pillow and took out he second pistol which they had given her – just in case. This she stowed away in her right pocket. She was ready.

Outside, the streets in Petrograd's Ochra slum quarter were cheerless. People looked shabby and undernourished. There were black marketeers, gaze wary, constantly on the lookout for the police, everywhere. At the corner, a whore who couldn't have been more than thirteen, had her hand inside a sailor's flies, smoking a cigarette at the same time, her white face set in a bored pout.

The woman stopped at a tea stall, its counter wet with spilled tea, to let a patrol of the Red Army march by. Some of the soldiers wore boots, but most were in wooden clogs. Routinely they cried 'peace' and 'land'. They did so without conviction.

A drunk staggered by her, waving a bottle of vodka and was sick over the counter. She shuddered. Ever since the Revolution, Petrograd had been like this – corrupt, vice-ridden, dirty, and disgusting. *'Boshe moi,'* she whispered to herself fervently, 'if I can only help to change it this day.' She went on.

An armoured car crawled by. Its hatch was closed and its machine gun swung from side to side like the snout of some primeval monster seeking out its prey. Hastily a group of deserters from the Red Army, selling sunflower seeds, scattered and ran for cover.

She turned a corner. In front of her there were squat, dirty-looking men in frock coats, long black curls protruding from beneath their shovel hats. With them were their women, fat and blousy, wearing yellow wigs to hide their shaven heads, suckling their children from their big dangling dugs.

The woman's nose wrinkled in disgust. *'Zhid,'* she said to herself, 'Yids!' They were the cause of all Russia's misfortunes. Why, weren't half the commissars in Lenin's government Yids? She and the rest of the Black Hundred should have killed more of them before the Revolution. Then Mother Russia would have been saved. She went on.

She walked on, the cold mud already seeping into her poor-quality Cheka boots. She didn't notice. Her mind was too full of her task. A tram clattered by. It was packed with peasants, clerks in bowlers and Red Army soldiers carrying bayoneted rifles. They yelled happily at passers-by and one of them made an obscene gesture with his finger to her. She looked hard at him and told herself in the old days her father, the Count, would have had the man flogged with a knout for even having looked at an aristocratic lady. Now all was 'free love'. The Reds had the morals of the farmyard. Everyone knew that.

Ten minutes later she reached her destination, the Smolny Institute, which was the Petrograd HQ of the Cheka. Once, as a girl, she had climbed the façade of the Institute, much to the delight of her fellow pupils and the horror of the lady principal. She had tweaked her ear and told her she'd come to a bad end. Then the principal had asked her what had happened to her stays as if that had been of great importance. She gave a little sigh. That had been in what seemed another age, when the sun had always shone and she had been blissfully happy. *He* had helped to change all that. That was why he would have to die.

She waited till an Army truck had clattered past. As always it bore the same silly legend, 'All Power to the People'. In fact the people had no power whatsoever. That lay in the hands of the tyrant Lenin and his Jews.

There was a guard on the front door of the Institute, busy checking the passes of all those who entered the building. She nodded her approval. That would keep him occupied. She crossed the street and stole round the back of the building. From inside she could hear the muted clatter of a typewriter, and a telephone bell was ringing urgently. But all the windows were closed and no one was in sight. She cast an urgent look to left and right. Nobody! She could start.

She reached up and caught hold of an ornamental iron trough, which in the days she had attended school there had contained flowers. She felt the bars, cold and clammy, and rested her weight on them. They held. It was a start. Seconds later she was balanced on the iron trough, reaching upwards for a narrow ledge which would be her next hold. Slowly, metre by metre, balancing with difficulty on the wet, crumbling façade, she worked herself on to the second floor where he had an office.

She reached the narrow ornamental ledge which ran right round the building. That was her objective. She could work her way along it to his room. For a few moments she balanced herself on it to regain her breath and steady herself. The drop now was a good twenty metres. She daren't look down, but that iron will of hers made her go on.

Slowly, very slowly, she started to edge herself along the ledge, body pressed close to the wall, her breath coming in short, harsh gasps. By now her body was soaked in a cold sweat, her heart beating like a trip-hammer. Still she forced herself to go on. Once a little piece of the stone wall broke off and went clattering to the ground below. She halted, tense with shock. Nothing happened. No one had heard the fall. She went on.

A few minutes later she had made it. There was his room. She peered through the window cautiously. The room was unlit and empty, as they had told her it would be. Fanatic for work as her victim-to-be was, he was also not very punctual. She still had time.

Gingerly, the muscles of her right leg aflame with pain from the effort of balancing on the narrow ledge, she took out the package which they had prepared for her, for their spies had told them that the window was always kept locked. Carefully she unrolled the piece of thick brown packing paper, already smeared with treacle. She pasted it on the pane of the window, closest to the catch. She smoothed it and waited now for one of the blue-and-yellow trams to pass which ran up and down the street below. She heard one coming down the line with the usual clatter of steel wheels on the rusting track. Out came the revolver. She held it by the muzzle. Hardly daring to breathe now and tense with excitement, she waited till it was directly below and then she swung the revolver. The glass shattered immediately, almost without noise. She grinned and breathed out hard. She'd done it!

Moments later she had opened the catch and was inside. She pulled the shabby, dirty curtain a little so that it hid the shattered pane and then looked around the office, its sole decoration a large picture of the tyrant Lenin, chin thrust out, hand raised as he harangued a crowd. She spat on the floor. Well, he was on his deathbed at least. Soon it would be the turn of his successor to die – *violently* – if she had her way.

For a moment she hesitated. Should she hide? If so, where? Then she whispered to herself, 'Why fool yourself? You're not going to live anyway. Sit in his chair. Wait for him there. Shoot him as he comes through the door and have done with it.' She nodded and lowered herself into his chair. Then she placed the two revolvers on the desk close to her hands, and waited...

Two doors away, Aronson, tall, blond and muscular, waited impatiently. As always, the head of the Petrograd Cheka had a myriad things to do, but first he had to wait to report to Trotsky, the Commissar for Foreign Affairs, who preferred to conduct his business from Petrograd and not Moscow; and as always, Lenin's designated successor was late.

This January, Aronson was a worried man.

With Lenin on his deathbed, anything could happen in his beloved Russia. It was obvious that Stalin wanted power for himself. The pockmarked ex-bank robber, who was now the Party's General Secretary, simply wouldn't let Trotsky take over the country without a fight. That could lead to all sorts of complications. Already Petrograd was flooded with rumours. A right-wing revolution was being planned. The Western Allies, Britain, France and America, were preparing to intervene in Russian affairs for a second time, just as they had done in 1918. Germany was ready to grab huge chunks of Russian territory, as she had in 1917, once the Soviet state started to tremble and fall...

Aronson sighed. He loved 'Holy Mother Russia' fervently. In his own time, Russia had been ruled by fools, even by traitors like the last Tsarina, whose first loyalty had been to her own country, Germany. Then there had been that weak-kneed liberal Kerensky who had overthrown the Tsar. He had been thrown out by the Mongol Lenin, who had spent most of his life abroad, sabotaging their noble country. But Russia would survive Lenin, Stalin and Trotsky as well, because there were men like him who loved the black earth of Mother Russia and its ordinary people, drunken, lazy and ignorant as most of them were. Such men, Aronson told himself, didn't want glory for themselves or power. They simply wanted the welfare of Russia and now, it seemed, trouble loomed ahead once again.

There was a soft tap on the door. Ilona, from the radio room in the cellar, entered. She was one of his current mistresses and also his spy in the radio room.

'Yes?' he asked the striking blonde, with her green eyes and splendid figure.

She blew him a kiss and said, 'This has just been picked up. Between the German Embassy in London and their Naval Intelligence HQ in Flensburg.' She came over to his desk, placed the slip of paper in his hand and in the same instant squeezed his penis with the other.

He laughed. 'Well, that cheered me up a bit, Ilona. But it is a bit early – and I'm expecting him – you know who – at any minute.' His smile vanished as he read the decipher of the coded German message. 'Smith and Bird sighted at Windsor. Believed received by the King.'

She looked down at him. 'Does it mean much?' she asked.

He didn't answer for a few moments. Then

52

he said, 'It is not wise to know too much, Ilona. I'll tell you this much, however. Wherever these two young Englishmen have turned up in the last few years it has always meant trouble for Mother Russia.'

Her exciting green eyes sparkled at his use of 'Mother Russia' instead of the obligatory 'Soviet State'. She always told herself that he wasn't really a Communist, but some kind of reactionary, secretly plotting against the Soviets. And she knew, too, he wasn't one of the hated Jews, even though his name sounded Jewish. She had learned that the first time she had gone to bed with him. She frowned. But that was about all she knew. Aronson was a man of mystery.

'*Mir boudit!*' The slogan being yelled below by the Red Guards startled the two of them. '*Peace is coming!*' it echoed up and down the gloomy corridors.

'Trotsky,' Aronson said. 'You'd better go.'

'*Zhid!*' she said contemptuously. 'Bronstein, that's his real name.'

He grinned and waved his hand. 'Off you go, my pretty little anti-Semite.'

Hastily she bent and gave his penis another delightful squeeze and then fled.

The Commissar for Foreign Affairs came striding down the corridor, followed by his bodyguard and the usual collection of fawning hangers-on. This morning he was wearing a military style leather tunic and cap and he had a pistol belt strapped around his ample waist. Aronson, watching him approach, told himself that despite the military garb and pistol, Trotsky's wispy goatee and pince-nez made him look like a provincial grocer or suburban pen-pusher.

Trotsky spotted the waiting Cheka chief. 'Comrade Aronson,' he snapped in that nervous, impatient manner of his which he cultivated to make it appear that he was a very, very busy man, weighed down by the cares of state. 'In my office … five minutes.' He opened the door. Next minute he staggered back, bleeding heavily from a sudden wound in the shoulder, and in an instant all was chaos and confusion…

Chapter Four

They had used the Bison and Dr Pox first. It was the usual treatment they gave women prisoners of the bourgeois class. The Bison was enormous, nearly two metres tall with shoulders like an ox but with the brain of a six-year-old child. He stared down at the woman strapped to the table naked, in blank uncomprehension, saliva dribbling down from the sides of his slack imbecile's mouth, making meaningless noises.

Aronson had nodded to Dr Pox, the old raddled whore they used to get Bison started. Expertly she undid the big man's flies and reached inside with her painted claws, cigarette held in one corner of her painted mouth, eyes screwed to slits with the smoke.

The Bison had whimpered with delight as she went to work on him with her cunning fingers, his breathing suddenly hectic. Then they had all gasped, even those who had seen the procedure before. 'Now I know why they call him Bison,' someone said in a hushed, awed whisper.

'He's ready,' Dr Pox said and took her hand away. She sucked at a cigarette and then, as if to prove that she had done her work well, she flicked at the Bison's enormous organ with thumb and finger. 'Hard as a rock,' she said almost proudly.

For his part, the Bison had simply stood there, looking down at the naked body of the woman strapped to the bench in the Cheka's cellar, her eyes filled with horror at the sight of the monster towering above her.

'*Horoscho,*' Aronson had ordered. 'Good. Get on with it.'

'*Davoi,*' Dr Pox had commanded. She had taken the Bison by that enormous penis of his and guided him so that its bulbous, blood-engorged tip had nudged her pubes. 'Go on, you idiot,' she had urged. 'Get on with it. Make her eyes pop, you fool.' She had laughed in that harsh, raucous manner of hers.

The Bison's moronic face had flushed scarlet. 'Yes?' he asked thickly.

'Yes,' Dr Pox had said and suddenly Aronson had realised, ancient whore that she was, who had probably serviced whole regiments of men in her time, that she was enjoying this systematic rape of the prisoner.

Still the Bison hesitated, as if he could not believe he was going to be allowed to do this. On the bench the would-be assassin wriggled and squirmed furiously, trying to break her bonds, her eyes full of fear and loathing.

'You know what they say about big men,' Dr Pox screeched. 'They're like big houses. The bottom floor is the worst furnished. But not in the Bison's case.' She laughed coarsely. 'Go on, give it to her. We've got things to do.'

She gave him a push and he tumbled on her.

The woman screamed with agony as the great organ entered her frail body. Her spine arched like a taut bowstring and a wild shiver went right through her, as he began to pump himself in and out of her, his breath coming in great hectic gasps.

Aronson turned away. He couldn't look any longer, but the others continued to stare, fascinated by the sight of the great beast of a man thrusting himself into the prisoner. It was a wretched business, he told himself, but it had to be done. Trotsky, fortunately, hadn't been badly hurt. He'd be up and about within the week. Still, it was a week that that Georgian savage Stalin in Moscow might well use to his own advantage. He had to know what the woman had hoped to achieve with Trotsky's death and who her backers were.

On the bench the woman was screaming and writhing frantically, trying to drag her loins away from the imbecile, as he pumped away at her, his rump glistening with sweat, while Dr Pox cackled, 'Go on, Bison dick it into her – *hard!*'

Suddenly the Bison gasped and let out an almost female shriek. He staggered back, trousers around his ankles absurdly, face crimson, the sweat dripping down his cheeks in opaque pearls. Dr Pox slapped him playfully across his broad rump and said, 'There you are, you naughty boy. Put it away now till next time.'

Obediently, still sobbing for breath, his massive chest heaving, as if he had just run a great race, the Bison had done as he was commanded. The interrogation could begin.

He had had her battered, naked body covered with a blanket. Her hands had been released and someone had brought her a pepper vodka, which she had sipped and coughed, the tears streaming down her bruised face all the while. Aronson had waited patiently enough for her to finish, for he guessed her spirit had been broken by the brutal rape. There would be no need to frighten her any more.

When she was finished, he took the glass from her and said, 'Do you want a cigarette?' His voice was soft and controlled.

She looked at him almost gratefully. 'Yes, please, if I can.'

He took out one of the long *papiroki*, which cost a fortune on Petrograd's black market, lit it and handed it to her. 'There you are,' he said gently.

He let her take a few puffs before asking in

the same quiet voice, 'What did you hope to gain by the assassination of Comrade Trotsky, comrade? You must know our system is established now. There is no hope for you of the bourgeoisie – you pale hands.' He used the peasant term of contempt for those who had never dirtied their hands with manual labour. 'The old regime is finished. It can never be restored.'

He looked down at her in the harsh yellow light that came from the naked bulb above their heads. Somewhere a man was groaning in agony, crying in between moans, 'I never did … honest, comrade, I never did.' Aronson frowned. One of the Cheka was torturing someone unnecessarily long. His motto was always one sharp shock, such as the rape he had just witnessed and that usually did the trick. After that there was no need for any more brutality. 'Well?' he demanded.

She took the cigarette out of her mouth with a hand that shook badly. 'We do not believe that,' she said softly but defiantly.

'You were with the Black Hundred, weren't you?' Aronson ventured a guess. He meant the prewar organisation of right-wingers who had assassinated Jews.

He caught the quick look in her eyes and knew he had struck gold. 'Was it because

Comrade Trotsky is a Jew? Was that the reason you attempted to kill him?'

'No,' she answered, 'not just because he was a Jew.' She hesitated and Aronson knew he must not let her stop. She might well clam up then.

'Why then?' he barked a little sharply.

His change of tone surprised her, for she stuttered, 'We believe in the return of the Little Father.'

'He is long dead, these five years. Do you believe in ghosts, comrade?' he sneered. 'I didn't think that even the Black Hundred reactionaries were that stupid.'

'We're not stupid,' she retorted, with a little of her old spirit animating her ashen face. 'We know that all of them did not die – were murdered – at Ekaterinburg.'

Aronson caught his breath. He knew something about the murder of the Tsar and the Imperial family at the remote Siberian town, but there had always been conflicting reports of what had happened. Some said the royal family had been thrown down a mineshaft and covered with lime. Others maintained that they had been weighted down and thrown in a swamp. No one, even at Cheka HQ, knew exactly what had happened because the killers had long vanished, some captured by the Whites when they had taken Ekaterinburg, others killed in the Civil War. Could there be a slight chance that one of the Romanovs had survived?

'Tell me more,' he barked and added swiftly, 'remember, if you lie or attempt to hide anything I can bring that hulk in to you once more.'

She cowered under the rough blanket. 'No, please not *that!* I couldn't stand that again … that beast with his…' She broke off, her eyes looking up at him pleadingly.

'Speak then.' He looked threateningly at her. 'What else do you know? Where is this supposed Romanov survivor, eh?'

'I am speaking the truth. I honestly don't know where. We of the Black Hundred just know that one exists.'

Aronson did some quick thinking. 'The Tsarevich would have died anyway by now even if he had survived the killings,' he snapped. 'He would not have lasted beyond the age of fourteen with that killing disease of his – haemophilia. If one of the grand duchesses had survived she would hardly be a rallying point for your people. So who are we talking about, woman, eh?'

'Grand Duke Serge,' she said simply, the knowledge growing within her that she could say no more, or everything and everybody would be betrayed. She had failed to kill the monster Trotsky which would have been the first great step; she deserved to die.

'Grand Duke Serge,' Aronson repeated in surprise. 'I have never heard of him. No such person exists. Now, don't play around with me. Speak up and tell the truth.'

She bent her head so that the man couldn't see the new look of determination in her eyes. 'I will,' she said humbly, as if her spirit were completely broken. 'But could I go to the privy first? I need to make water – and I am bleeding.' She drew the blanket back to show him the blood trickling down the inside of her legs.

'All right,' he snapped impatiently, though in fact he felt a little sorry for her. She was a brave woman, who had fought for the wrong cause. 'But hurry it up. There is a privy just outside the door.'

'Thank you. You are kind.' She took a last look at the tall blond interrogator, as if trying to assess what he might do now. But Aronson was too busy mulling over what she had just said about this Grand Duke Serge to notice the look. Draping the blanket about her, she went out, while he waited there, knowing there was no escape for her; every exit was guarded by an armed Cheka policeman.

Aronson told himself that in the coming power struggle between the wounded Trotsky and Stalin, with the country on the verge of starvation, there might well be a great deal of support for some new Romanov, even if he were a fake. He knew his Russians. They were attracted to the mystic, the unusual, anything and anybody which offered hope: a release from their normal miserable existence. A new Romanov could well provide a rallying cry for the mob, especially if that Romanov was backed up by those famed Horsemen of St George, those English sovereigns, which had more power to subvert and destroy than any English army that he knew of. Suddenly he remembered the signal that Ilona had brought him just before Trotsky had been wounded. Were those two notorious English troublemakers, Smith and Bird, involved in this strange business? After all, they had helped to destroy the power of the Red Fleet at Kronstadt back in 1918. Then there had been Poland, which they had helped to save from the Germans, turning that country into an implacable enemy of Mother Russia.

Aronson frowned. He had to get to the bottom of this nasty business – and soon.

Lenin was on his deathbed. Since his last stroke, the Soviet dictator had not spoken for weeks. When the balloon went up and the power struggle commenced, he wanted to be ready for every eventuality.

Suddenly, startlingly, the crash of broken glass and a shrill scream broke into his anxious reverie. He knew immediately, with the clarity of a vision, what had happened. '*Boshe moi!*' he cried and ran to the door. Clerks and cops were running up the stairs. A typist, verging on hysteria, was shouting, 'She just threw herself out … I couldn't stop her… Honestly, she just threw herself…'

Aronson did not bother to climb the stairs. He knew where she would be. She had climbed the stairs and thrown herself out of a window. It was the classic suicide pattern. He went to the main door, ignoring the clenched fist salute of the sentries. His mind was on other things. He walked around to where the little crowd had already gathered, staring numbly at something he could not yet see. 'Comrades, out of the way,' he commanded and they parted. The big blond man had a natural air of authority about him and everyone was scared of the Cheka secret police.

He looked down at the woman, naked, her

body completely exposed, sprawled out in the unnatural, extravagant posture of those done violently to death. He supposed she had been pretty once. Now she was dead in the cold mud, a thin trickle of blood coming from her nostrils. He took off his tunic and draped it over her lower body.

Out over the River Neva a thin fog had started to drift in, wrapping itself around the buildings which Peter the Great, who had given his name to this city, had built like a silent grey cat. Aronson stared hard at it, trying to penetrate it, wondering what mystery lay out there. Then he turned and walked slowly and thoughtfully back inside. 'Clear her away,' he said quietly to the sentries at the door. He saw Ilona. She was standing at the head of the stairs. She had been crying. He could see that. She looked at him directly. He did not return the look. There would be plenty of weeping before this bad business was over, he told himself, and then he went into his office. He locked the door and sat there in silence, smoking cigarette after cigarette: a man of mystery, trying to unravel a mystery.

Chapter Five

'It's all deuced mysterious,' C said slowly, as if he were considering every word, while Smith and Bird waited expectantly.

As usual they had been passed through the myriad passages which made up the rabbit warren which was the Secret Service's HQ at 21 Queen Anne's Gate. Now they sat opposite the man who knew more of the Empire's secrets than any other living creature.

C's room was large, but due to some trick of the lighting everything in it seemed to appear in silhouette. A line of telephones on extensions stood to the left of the great oak desk, which reputedly had once belonged to Nelson himself. To the right there was a smaller desk littered with maps, models of aeroplanes and submarines, plus a row of bottles which suggested chemical experiments. This evidence of scientific investigation seemed to Smith only to heighten the overpowering atmosphere of strangeness and mystery.

C stared hard at the two of them through

his gold-rimmed monocle and continued, as the muted sound of London's traffic below came in through the window. 'Before the war the Tsar had a long-standing affair with a famous ballerina from the Bolshoi – that's a ballet theatre,' he added, as if he thought they might not know what the name signified.

'You mean where those chaps with curls and no trousers swan around, sir?' Dickie Bird said cheekily, before Smith could stop him.

But irony was wasted on C. 'Yes, Bird, that's the sort of place. Not the sort of place I would care to visit, I can tell you, but then the Russkis are a funny lot.'

Inwardly Smith grinned. C, the stern old ex-naval captain, would be the last person he would expect to visit the ballet, 'Where there are loose women showing their knickers and nancy boys prancing about all over the place,' he told himself.

C continued. 'To cut a long story short, the Tsar married the dancer-woman – morganatically, of course – and in due course she bore him a child, a son, named, I believe,' he glanced down at the paper in front of him, 'Serge. Now according to the most reliable information our service could obtain, the Bolos murdered the whole of the Romanov family, with the exception of this boy, who must now be in the region of ten or twelve.'

Smith shot Dickie Bird a swift glance. It read– 'So that was what the King-Emperor was on about.'

Dickie nodded his agreement as C glanced down at the paper in front of him once more.

Smith studied the balding little man, of whom it was said that when he had been in France on a mission during the Great War, he had been trapped under his wrecked automobile after a bad accident. Thereupon he had cold-bloodedly cut off his own mangled leg with his penknife and had crawled to the safety of his own lines with the German mounted Uhlans after him. Smith could well believe the tale. There was something totally hard about the head of the Secret Service.

'Somehow that boy survived,' C continued. 'That means he is the pretender to the Russian throne. Now we have reliable information from Finland that he and an attendant are making their way to Petrograd.' He rose and hobbled over to the large map of Russia and the Baltic on the wall, using his malacca cane to give him more support, the joint of his wooden leg squeaking audibly. He tapped the great Russian port on the map. 'Well, you two chaps know the approach to Petrograd well enough. But there'd be no chance you could do again what you did in 1918. The Russkis have got the place well sewn up by now. However,' he paused and stared hard at them, 'if that child could be brought out and across to the Finnish port of Viborg here...'

'–You want us to bring him out, sir,' Smith beat C to it, 'and then go all about through the Baltic before the Russkis can react?'

'Exactly, Smith,' C said, staring at Smith's tough, handsome face and telling himself that Common Smith VC was one of those find young Englishmen who kept the Empire going; and with trouble everywhere from India to Ireland, the old country certainly needed plenty of that type.

'But what's so important, sir, about this youth?' Dickie Bird asked, puzzled.

'Well, for one thing the King-Emperor doesn't want the last living Romanov to be killed by those Red brutes. He feels he did wrong in refusing permission for the Russian royal family to come to England back in '18.' C lowered his voice a little. 'But there's a much more important reason than that. The Cabinet wants to be in a position to take a hand in Russian affairs when that monster

Lenin dies and the whole damned Soviet state falls apart.'

'Do you think it will, sir?' Smith asked quickly.

'Our people there seem to think so. They say there are so many rivals for Lenin's position that there's bound to be fighting, perhaps even civil war. That means that, with a bit of luck, there'll be an end to this damned Communist rubbish once and for all. It has poisoned half the world as it is. Even our own people are getting far too bolshy.'

Smith and Bird nodded their agreement. C was right, of course. Since the war there had been demands to abolish the monarchy. There had been strike after strike, with even the police going on strike for a short while. Communism had a lot to answer for.

'So if we have the last of the Romanovs safely over here, so the Cabinet thinks, we can recommend him to the mass of the Russian people as the new ruler. In essence, you two,' C looked hard at them, as if seeing them for the very first time, 'you are going to be throne-makers!'

Smith whistled softly and Dickie Bird exclaimed, 'Oh, my sainted aunt! Bit like the *Prisoner of Zenda* thing, what, sir?'

'Not exactly,' C answered coldly, and

70

Smith told himself C had probably not read a book since he left Dartmouth forty-odd years before. 'It is, therefore, the most important mission you have ever undertaken for me. It is one that might influence the future of Europe, perhaps even the world. An end to that evil plague which is sweeping the globe – *Communism!*'

C let his words sink in before he continued. 'Now, your first task is to get yourself and the *Swordfish* to Finland, Smith. It's not going to be easy. You're well known to our enemies abroad by now. So we must smuggle you, the crew and the *Swordfish* out of the country.'

'*Smuggle?*' Bird and Smith echoed as one.

'Yes. My service has hired a Swedish tramp steamer. It normally transports timber from Swedish ports to Hull and brings back whatever cargo it can find. Well, when it sails in forty-eight hours' time, you chaps will be on board.' He gave them a wintry smile, pleased with himself that he had surprised the two young officers. 'Oh yes,' he chortled, 'there is still life in the old dog yet, you know. Now,' he went on, 'once you have been offloaded at Viborg, you will be contacted.' C hesitated, seemingly suddenly uncertain. 'Your contact man is a strange person. He's the best in the field. Been with us for nearly thirty years now. Worked for us all over the show.' He frowned. 'But I don't know whether I can altogether trust him. He's got his fingers in too many pies.' Then he added, as if the remark explained everything, 'He calls himself Reilly, as if he were Irish, but he's a Jew of course.'

'Will this – er – Reilly chap,' Smith said, 'smuggle the Romanov boy out of Russia, sir? Is that the plan?'

Again C was strangely hesitant for him. 'Reilly plays with his cards close to his chest,' he said. 'He says it's better that way. Then there is less chance that he will be betrayed, he always maintains. So I don't really know. Once he makes contact with you, Reilly will be in charge.'

'I see, sir,' Smith said. Now it was his turn to frown. He didn't like the idea of being under the command of a civilian, and a spy at that. He liked to make his own decisions, especially where the *Swordfish* and her loyal crew were concerned.

'Now then, you two,' C rose to his feet, indicating that the briefing was nearly over, 'I want you to remember this. Don't venture *one foot* into Russia itself; you are both dead men if they catch you in that accursed coun-

72

try. Remember this as well, be on your guard with Reilly. He is unpredictable and dangerous, very dangerous.' C forced a wintry smile and held out his hand to Smith. 'Godspeed, my boy, and best of luck.'

Smith took the Secret Service chief's hand and found it surprisingly firm and hard for such an old man.

Then it was Dickie Bird's turn. A moment later C pressed the button which changed the light that hung outside his door from red to green to indicate that he was no longer in conference and they went out.

But for a moment or two C did not take up his fountain pen to begin signing letters in green ink, the symbol of his high office. Instead he slumped there, staring gloomily at the first sad flakes of snow, drifting down outside.

He knew for certain Reilly was a murderer who had killed his wife's first husband to obtain that old man's young wife and fortune. Since then he had killed many men, perhaps not always in the interest of the Service, but then he had powerful patrons in the form of Winston Churchill and his father-in-law, Sir H.M. Hozier. He was greedy too, very greedy. But was he a traitor? What if this whole business with the startling discovery of the Tsar's heir, six years after the Tsar had been murdered, was simply a trick to lure the two best-hated Englishmen in the Soviet state back to that country? Had he just sent Smith and Bird to their deaths?

Eventually, C shook his head and gave up. He began to sign his letters, as outside the snow started to come down in a white stream, almost hiding the two heavy-set men in long, foreign-looking overcoats who were hiding in the doorway opposite. *'Da sind sie, Kurt,'* the bigger of the two hissed.

His companion nodded. *'Los,'* he said.

Together, hands dug deep into the pockets of their coats, bodies bent against the flying snow, they started to follow the two old friends as they trudged up the street, trying to find a taxi to take them to King's Cross.

Chapter Six

The next twenty-four hours passed in hectic activity. At their base in the remote East Yorkshire village of Withernsea – 'the arsehole of the world', as Ginger Kerrigan was wont to call it – the crew of the *Sword-*

fish set about preparing for their mission to Finland. Supplies from nearby Hull were taken on board – extra fuel for the greedy Thorneycroft engines, more ammunition for the Lewis guns, extra winter clothing, including great leather, fur-lined coats which came down to their ankles…

CPO Ferguson, accompanied by Ginger Kerrigan and his running mate, big fat Billy Bennett, were detailed to go to Leeds to pick up 5000 sovereigns, those 'Horsemen of St George' that they might need to bribe the locals. For all the crew knew that, unlike true Englishmen, foreigners always liked to have 'their palms greased'. Foreigners were like that.

'What about some decent grub when we get there?' Billy Bennett asked eagerly, licking his lips as if in anticipation. 'Nice old meat pie with peas, lashings of gravy, Chiefie.'

Ginger Kerrigan looked at his old comrade scornfully. 'I don't know, blubber guts. Don't you ever think of higher things, like a bit o' grumble and grunt?'

For his part, CPO Ferguson had looked at the two of them severely and had said in that dour Scots manner of his, 'There'll be nae o' yon fornication while I'm in charge.'

Meanwhile Smith and Dickie Bird pored

over maps of the Baltic and Finland, while outside the snow fell out of the sky over the North Sea as if it would never stop. 'As I see it, Dickie,' Smith said, 'not only can we expect trouble from the Russkis, but we might have a run in with von Horn's Huns.' He meant *Fregattenkapitan* von Horn, the perverted head of the illegal German Naval Intelligence Division. 'He's been after our blood since '21. If he can put a spoke in the wheel, he'll do it.'

'How right you are,' Dickie Bird agreed heartily. 'Can't trust the Huns.'

Smith stared at the whirling snowflakes sombrely, listening to the mournful sound of the local lighthouse's foghorn. 'I wouldn't put it past that man betraying us to the Russkis if he could. They say the Reds and Huns are already working secretly together in military matters.'

Dickie Bird nodded and sipped reflectively at his pink gin. 'So what are we going to do, old bean?' he asked.

'We'll change C's plan a little,' Smith answered.

'How?'

'Like this. If we could get the *Swordfish* boxed up, which shouldn't be too difficult, and placed on the deck of this Swedish timber ship as super cargo, she shouldn't arouse any suspicion as we pass through the Kattegat – here – into the Baltic. I mean the Huns really control the entrance into the Baltic. So if they're nosey, what will they see? Crates, that's all.'

'What ho, Smithie!' Dickie cried. 'Splendid wheeze!'

'I think so. Even if the Hun customs police do stop us, the Swedes can say they're heading for Stockholm or somewhere like that.'

Together they studied the map carefully, following the direct route across the Gulf of Bothnia until they came to the Finnish port of Abo, north of Helsingfors. 'According to this map,' Smith said slowly, 'There's a railway running southeast from Abo, branching off to Helsingfors. The other goes off into the relatively uninhabited interior to Vyborg. We could transport the *Swordfish*, crated up as I've suggested, by rail, to our port of operation.'

Dickie Bird whistled softly. 'If it can be done, it sounds a deucedly splendid idea to me. Then if the Huns and the jolly old Bolos are looking for us, we spend less time at sea in the Baltic.'

'Exactly.'

The more he thought about it, the more

Smith liked the idea, and in the end he telephoned C to ask his permission. C was his usual brisk self. 'Sleep on it, Common Smith. Let you know p.d.q. though.' The phone went dead.

Two hours later the ancient postie who had lost a leg at Loos came pedalling, cursing and skidding down the promenade to where the crew of the *Swordfish* were housed in Withersea's Commercial Hotel, bearing a telegram. Knocking the snow off his helmet, he handed the message over and said, 'Ruddy brass monkey weather out there, gentlemen. 'Taint fit fer a 'uman.'

Smith knew what that meant. He slipped his hand in his pocket and took out a three-penny bit. 'Here you are, postie, treat yourself to a nip. But don't get caught by the bobby. Don't want you charged for the drunken driving of a bike.'

The ancient postie grinned, touched his helmet in salute and said, 'Old Charlie Thompson'll have to get up a bit earlier in the morning to catch me.' Then he was gone and Smith tore open the buff envelope.

The message was simple and short. *Agreed change,* it read. *Will be done.*

There was no signature.

The next morning, Smith assembled the

men in the snug of the Commercial Hotel. They came in informally, for he had drummed into them that they were no longer members of the Royal Navy, but ordinary merchant seamen, all except CPO Ferguson. After thirty years in the RN he couldn't forget the habits of a lifetime. So when Smith said, 'All right, lads, sit down. I've got something to tell you,' Ferguson glared at the *Swordfish's* crew and barked, 'Mind, ye'll all sit to attention when the officer speaks.'

'All right, Chiefie,' Dickie Bird tried to appease him. 'Keep it down to a dull roar. We don't want all of jolly old Withernsea knowin' what we're about.'

Ferguson looked at him hard with those grey eyes of his, but said nothing.

'Well, we're off back to the Baltic,' Smith commenced, as outside the wind howled and rattled the snug's windows and the snow continued to fall in a white fury. 'It's going to be a bit nip-and-tuck.'

'We're used to that, sir,' Ginger Kerrigan said, and taking the cigarette end from behind his right ear, lit it while Ferguson glared at him. 'As long as us lads have their Woodbines, wallop and a bit of the old other now and agen, we're happy.'

'Don't forget the grub,' Billy Bennett

chimed in. 'Bloke's got to have a bite to eat now and agen.'

Ferguson's glare intensified. 'Hold yer stupid whuish!' he barked. 'Can ye no see the officer's wanting to get on?'

'Thanks, Chiefie,' Smith said and continued, briefing them on the mission and at the same time telling himself what a decent and loyal bunch of fellows they were. Men of no education with few prospects, they were prepared to risk their lives for King and Country on a wage of a few shillings a week. His heart went out to them. 'Well,' he concluded, 'you can see the mission is very important. But it's very dangerous. You're all volunteers and any one of you who doesn't think he can go ahead, I won't hold it against him.' He waited while CPO Ferguson glared at the crew, as if daring any of them to withdraw.

It was Sparks, the youngest of the crew, who had lost an eye in the Zeebrugge Raid of 1918, who now expressed the crew's attitude. He rose and said confidently, 'I think I can speak for the rest of the lads, sir, when I say, we'll get the little bastard back – the Russki one – come hell or high water!' He grinned and the men grinned back.

Dickie Bird cried, 'Well spoken, Sparks.

Now I'll also speak – for the wardroom.' He flashed a glance at Smith. 'I think we'll splice the mainbrace a little early this cold and wintry day, what!'

CPO Ferguson looked shocked. 'Ye'll be no taking the strong waters at eleven o'clock o' the morning, sir!' he protested.

'You betcha, chiefie,' Dickie Bird chortled, using the latest American expression, which had come in with the Charleston, the newest dance rage in Mayfair. The next moment he opened the hatch to the bar and shouted happily to the landlord, 'Closed or not, land-lord, we're coming through for drinkies, what!'

It was half an hour later when all of them, even CPO Ferguson, were mellow and happy with a couple of tots of neat rum inside them, that it happened. They were on their way down the incline on the promenade to where the *Swordfish* was berthed, fighting the raging snowstorm, when there was a sudden rumbling behind them. At first none of them paid any attention to the noise; they were concentrating on the snow, which had made the road slippery. By chance Smith forced himself to turn round to look up the incline. In an instant he realised they were in trouble.

81

A lorry, packed with what looked like cylinders, was trundling towards them, with its headlights off – and no driver in the cab! 'A runaway!' he yelled with all his strength. 'Someone forgot to put the blocks under its wheels... *Look out!*'

Madly they fought to get out of the way of the huge lorry bearing down on them. To his horror Smith saw, as the men sprang onto the pavement and off the road, that if it wasn't stopped, the lorry would hit the balustrade which ran the length of the promenade. He realised at that same moment, that the tall iron bottles at the back might well explode with disastrous results.

Face tense and expectant, he waited till the lorry came parallel with him. 'Look out, Mr Smith!' CPO Ferguson yelled in alarm. 'Yon rulley–' But de Vere Smith wasn't listening. He hurled himself upwards and grabbed the cab's brass door handle. With one and the same movement, he wrenched it open and forced himself inside. He grabbed for the big wheel. Now the balustrade was only feet away. He jerked it to the left. At the same time he grabbed frantically for the brake lever. He pulled it hard. Nothing happened. *The brakes wouldn't work!*

Now he was trundling down the promenade, half-blinded by the driving snow, the wheels skidding from side to side. Cursing madly, he changed down. But the change had little effect. The big lorry's speed was not diminishing on the slope. Smith made a snap decision. Just ahead to his right was a gap where the council's workmen had knocked off repairing the damaged balustrade because of the raging snowstorm. Down below there were the sands, made wet and slushy by the receding tide and snow. He'd chance it.

Again he swung the wheel round. To the right this time. The lorry skidded. Next moment it shot through the gap, scattering loose bricks to left and right, and slammed into the sands seven feet below. Smith felt as if every bone in his body had been cracked. He tensed all the same for the great explosion to come. Nothing happened. Slowly, very slowly, the truck started to settle into the wet sand right up to its axle. 'Phew!' Smith gasped, realising that he was dripping with sweat. He slumped forward over the wheel, knowing even as he did that this wasn't an accident...

'You're right, sir,' the smart little CID man with the ferret eyes, from Hull, said. 'The lorry was stolen and the brake cable has been cut deliberately.' He stared down at the stranded lorry, with the waves now washing about it. 'If that little lot had exploded' – he indicated the iron flasks used for welding – 'there wouldn't have been much left of Withernsea.' He gave Smith a wintry smile. 'Mind you, some people in the East Riding around here would say that wouldn't be any great loss.'

'I know what you mean, we've spent three damned winters here. But who do you think could have done such a dastardly thing?'

By way of an answer, the CID man pulled a soggy matchbox out of his right pocket. 'Have a look at this, sir. The driver of the lorry says he's a non-smoker, so whoever nicked the thing must have left this behind.'

Curious, Smith took the matchbox in his hand. It wasn't the usual Swan Vesta yellow box common throughout the country. This box was a dingy blue with the word 'Mono-pol' written across its front. 'Swedish?' he asked.

The CID man shook his head. 'Look what's written below, sir,' he said.

Smith peered at the words and then read them out haltingly *'Streichholzer-hergestellt in Deutschland.'* He looked up at the CID man sharply. 'Made by the Huns?'

He nodded. 'Exactly, sir, German. It looks

very much as if somebody from that country doesn't like you and your crew.' He touched his hand to his trilby and turned to go. Then he changed his mind and said over his shoulder, 'If I was you, sir, I'd watch my back.' Then he was gone, trudging through the new snow.

Chapter Seven

'*Verdammte Scheisse!*' *Fregattenkapitan* von Horn cursed angrily. 'Damned shit!' He threw the signal onto his desk, while the young radio officer watched him a little fearfully. 'So the English swine have got away with it yet again!'

He pushed back his chair and strode over to the window. A group of cadets, totally naked with steam rising from their lithe young bodies, were rolling about in the new snow under the orders of a brawny petty officer. Von Horn nodded his approval. For the sight of all those naked young bodies gave him considerable pleasure.

Watching him as he viewed the candidates engaged in their hardening up exercise, the young signals officer thought he had never seen such a sinister face as that of his commanding officer. Von Horn's face was small and soft underneath the white-blond hair, with thin lips that looked as if they might have been painted on, yet no paint could hide their cruelty. But it was von Horn's eyes which were the most evil. They were hooded and dark, as if they had no depth at all, with an expression of boundless sadism.

Von Horn forced himself to take his eyes off the naked boys rolling and whooping in the snow. He turned and faced the signals officer. 'So what do we know?'

The other man didn't answer, for he knew it was a rhetorical question.

'We know from the signals from London and elsewhere in their accursed England that – one,' he held up a well-manicured finger with its lacquered nail, 'that they have seen their king. Two, almost immediately thereafter the two of them' – again he held up another finger – 'saw the head of that infamous English Secret Service. Finally, three, they head for the place where that vessel of theirs is berthed and where unfortunately our plans to do away with them at long last misfired. Now' – he put down his hand and stared at the young officer with those frightening, evil eyes of his, saying – 'what does that suggest to you, *Herr Leutnant?*'

The signals officer felt himself flush slightly. He knew all about his CO's sexual inclinations. There had been whispered stories in the *kasino* about young men with painted lips and plucked eyebrows being smuggled into von Horn's quarters at night; and there was something sexual about von Horn's look now. God, he told himself, I hope he doesn't fancy *me!* 'Well, sir,' he stuttered uneasily, 'they are being sent on a mission ... and it must be an important one if they are received by their king.'

'*Genau,*' von Horn said. 'But what is that mission? In three devils' name what are those swine up to?'

The young signals officer hesitated then he chanced it. 'There's just one thing, sir, that might be of some significance.'

'Fire away, man,' von Horn said eagerly.

'Well, sir, over the last month the diplomatic wireless traffic between the English consulate and trade mission in Petrograd has increased considerably. The English diplomatic code is not difficult and our people cracked it last year. Most – nearly all these messages are routine. You know, promotions, trade figures and the like.'

Von Horn snapped his fingers impatiently. 'Yes, yes, get on with it.'

'Well, sir, but there is part of that traffic that we can't crack. The code used is not the diplomatic one. We suspect it is a code used by their military intelligence.'

Von Horn was thoughtful for a moment. Then he asked, 'Is there nothing you can tell me about these mysterious messages?'

'Only that they have increased in number, sir, over the last month and that they are preceded by a single letter, which we think is the letter "R".'

'*R!* Did you say "R"?' von Horn demanded excitedly.

'Yes, at least that is what we think the coded first sequence means,' the young signals officer said hesitantly. 'Naturally we can't be completely sure...' His voice trailed away to nothing. He could see that von Horn was no longer listening.

Von Horn's brain raced electrically. It had to be that infamous English agent 'Reilly'. Everyone in the intelligence business had heard of the Russian Jew who maintained he was an Irishman born in Tipperary. He was a crackshot who spoke several languages and had worked for the English for a very long time.

'Is there anything else, *Herr Fregatten-kapitan?*' the signals officer asked.

'Yes. Is there any way that our listening service can detect whether these coded messages are being sent on – to a different place from Petrograd?'

'Of course, sir. We have our people in Petrograd, too. We pass them the details of what we require and they can signal back what they have found out.'

'How long?' he demanded impatiently.

'Bit difficult to say, sir. But we might have the information today. An "R" signal was sent from London to Petrograd this very morning.'

'Then off you go,' von Horn ordered. 'Let me know the minute you find out. And yes, make our decoding people drop everything else. They have to give immediate priority to the breaking of one of these "R" signals, as you call them. Is that understood?'

'*Jawohl, Herr Fregattenkapitan.*' The young signals officer clicked to attention and went out hurriedly, leaving von Horn alone with his thoughts. It seemed to him that Reilly was still at large in Soviet Russia. There were two centres of power in that enormous country, and von Horn was sure Reilly would be operating from one of the two, either Petrograd or Moscow. Everyone knew that Lenin, the Soviet dictator, was dying in the latter place. Otherwise Russia, at the moment, was at peace; nothing much of import was happening. The balloon would go up once the dictator had died. Then the power struggle would commence. So why was Reilly receiving urgent coded messages now, *before* Lenin's death?

Von Horn frowned and walked to the window. A fat sailor, with his beribboned cap at the back of his head, cigarette hanging from the corner of his mouth was making a half-hearted attempt to clean a path free of snow. Between each push of the broom, he straightened up and rested on its handle. Von Horn shook his head. How slack everything had become under this new socialist republic. In the days of the Kaiser, a lazy sailor like that would have long been in the guardroom.

The thought made him attack the Reilly problem with new urgency. Germany must be made great again, and the only way to do that was to wreck the power of her enemies, France and England and in particular, Russia.

Something was going on in either Petrograd or Moscow which interested the damned English greatly. Hence the increased wireless traffic. Somehow it concerned those two young swine who had wrecked his plans often enough in the past. So one thing was for sure. To reach Petrograd on neutral waters outside the great Russian port, where their mission would surely commence, they'd sail into the Baltic. He clicked his fingers excitedly, face hard, set and determined. That's where he would take them.

They'd soon talk, once his men went to work on the Englishmen. Why, he had men who boasted they could make 'even a mummy spill the beans'. Then if whatever they were up to in Russia was in Germany's interest he'd exploit it. Mind made up, he reached for the red telephone, the one for emergencies. First he called the Water Police. Officially they were to check for illegal cargos and the like on Germany's rivers and coastal waters. In reality, the police were made up of ex-regular officers and petty officers, who carried out illegal paramilitary functions at sea now that Germany's navy had been cut so drastically by the victorious Western Allies at the Treaty of Versailles. Swiftly von Horn gave a description of the *Swordfish* and its two young officers, ordering, 'They are to be taken alive. Remember, like most Englishmen, they are treacherous and cunning. No

91

dirty trick is too low for them.'

He replaced the phone on its red cradle and glanced furtively around his office, as if he half expected someone to be lurking there, listening. Then when he was completely satisfied that he was really alone, he picked up the phone and said, 'Operator, get me this number in Stockholm.' He gave the operator the secret number and, listening to him dial it, he added, 'Don't listen in either, *Obermaat,* when you make the connection. This is *most* secret.'

Impatiently he waited for the call to come through. Outside, it had started to snow again. The fat sailor with the broom shrugged his chubby shoulders and gave up. He went back inside again. Von Horn shook his head.

The phone shrilled. Von Horn crossed the room and picked it up. 'Goering?' he asked. 'Captain Goering?'

The reply seemed to take a long time in coming and when it did, Goering's voice was slurred and lifeless. 'Yes,' he said, 'it's me. Goering.'

Von Horn cursed to himself. Captain Goering, the fighter ace who had been the last commander of the Richthofen Squadron at the end of the Great War and who had refused to surrender to the Allies then, was back on dope. After the failure of the Austrian Hitler's revolt in Munich he had fled to Sweden where his wife lived. Now he was obviously consoling himself with that damned cocaine he sniffed.

'Listen hard, Goering,' von Horn said, his normally feline voice harsh and incisive as he tried to force his words through the drug addict's haze. 'How many planes have you currently available?' He meant the remaining planes of the Richthofen Squadron which Goering had ordered to fly to Sweden when the Allies had ordered that the defeated Germany should possess no warplanes. For a while the neutral Swedes had empounded them, but in 1920, as money had changed hands and Sweden was pro-German, they had been released. Now they were kept on a small remote peninsula off the Baltic ready for unorthodox missions.

'Four,' Goering said thickly.

'With pilots?' von Horn snapped, telling himself it was probably time for Goering to snort another charge of 'coke' up his ruined nostrils.

'Yes. Why do you ask?' There was a note of interest in his voice.

'I have a mission for you.'

'Fire away,' Goering said.

Swiftly von Horn explained the situation and said, 'We're patrolling the mouth of the Baltic with our small boats. I'd like you to run constant patrols, too. Twenty-four hours a day if you can manage it.'

'Can do,' Goering answered, and then, 'What do we do if we sight them?'

'If they won't heave to, you will sink them,' von Horn said harshly.

Goering chuckled malevolently. 'That will give me the greatest of pleasure.'

'Good. That's all, Goering.'

The line went dead and von Horn put the phone down. He sat back in his chair. He had done all he could for the moment. Slowly, very slowly, an evil smile started to flit across his face. Suddenly he felt like a spider which had spun its web. Now his victims were beginning to gradually enter that web. It was a good feeling. This time there would be no escape for the damned Englishmen. On impulse he snapped his palm and fingers tightly together. *He had them!*

BOOK TWO

CROSS-COUNTRY

Chapter One

'Madame Discretion?' he asked politely.

The brothel owner looked hard at him. She was fat and old, her hair dyed with henna, and was clothed only in a pale yellow silk wrap through which he could see her hanging breasts. Wordlessly she held out her hand, the nails very long and painted a brilliant scarlet.

Obediently he handed her the little purse while the half-naked whores, most of them clad only in black silk stockings and garters and transparent gowns, watched in bored curiosity.

Madame Discretion took the purse, opened it, counted the gold sovereigns, then as an afterthought bit into the edge of each one of them. Finally she nodded her approval. *'Bon,'* she said throatily, *'venez avec moi, m'sieu.'*

Again obediently he followed her, his dark, cunning eyes missing nothing as they passed out of the *salon* and began to descend the stairs – the chains and the whips on the walls, the pornographic statues everywhere, the two-way mirrors through which voyeurs could watch the sexual antics of others. His observations told him that while Madame Discretion and her whores now serviced the new Communist masters of Russia, she had done the same for the aristocrats of the old regime who obviously had had more sophisticated tastes than the peasants who now inhabited the Kremlin.

She opened the door of what appeared to be the cellar. A whiff of stale, fetid air assailed his nostrils. Automatically he touched his right pocket where his revolver lay. Was he walking into a trap? The fat brothel owner saw the movement. She shook her head and one enormous dug, the nipple painted scarlet, fell out of her wrapper. *'Pas dangereux,'* she reassured him. *'Seulement difficil.'*

'Oui, je comprends, madame,' he answered in fluent French, one of the half a dozen languages he understood in addition to his native Yiddish.

She took a torch from the clamp next to the door and handed it to him, saying, *'Allez … vite.'*

He nodded his thanks and stepped inside the narrow entrance.

Carefully he started to make his way down the narrow tunnel. Here and there rats scurried away at his approach, their bodies magnified grotesquely in the light of the torch. Moisture dropped from the ceiling. Slime coated the walls and there was a mouldy stench everywhere that made him want to choke and spit. Still he persisted, telling himself that the couple had found a wonderful hiding place. Not even the Cheka would think of searching for them in a disused sewer under a brothel.

He blundered into a wall. For a moment he thought his progress had come to an end. But after groping his way a little, he found the turn in the passage and continued. Suddenly he stopped and thanked God for the torch. Twenty metres below, water foamed and bubbled as it rushed along a narrow brick passage. One step more and he would have fallen straight into it. 'May the saints help and save me!' he exclaimed in that faked Irish accent he always used when he spoke to himself. He looked down at it for a few moments, guessing that it had been used by the brothel to get rid of unwelcome visitors or whores who had gotten pregnant and were no longer of any use in their job. Russia had always been full of young peasant girls who thought the profession of prostitute was glamorous or a means of escape from the drudgery of farm work. There was always plenty of new recruits eager to take up the job.

Carefully, for the ground was slippery and wet, he crossed the gap and went on to where, in the yellow light of the torch, he could see the steps leading upwards. This must be their hiding place, he told himself and began to mount them carefully, trying to be as silent as possible. For even now he was prepared to find that the meeting might be a trap. After all, he had survived as long as he had by being constantly on the alert. Even when he was in bed with one of his current six mistresses, he always kept a loaded automatic under the pillow.

He came to the head of the stairs. A door barred his way. From underneath it there came a chink of light and he could hear a child's voice saying something in a soothing tone. It had to be them, he told himself. Still, all the same, he reached into his pocket and clicked the safety off his revolver.

He knocked softly. There was a sudden silence which lasted for a long moment. Then a cultivated voice asked a little fearfully, 'Is it you?'

'Yes,' he answered in Russian. 'It is I, Your Highness.'

A bolt was drawn back. A moment later the door was opened and, framed in the square of yellow light coming from the single naked bulb which illuminated the secret room, a boy stood. He might have been twelve and he was poorly dressed in a shabby smock and black breeches in the peasant fashion. But there was no mistaking that imperious look and those bright blue eyes, the eyes of his murdered father. 'Who *are* you?' he demanded. Again the accent was definitely not provincial Russian. It was cultured and aristocratic.

The man bowed. 'My name is Reilly, Your Highness. I am the representative of the British Secret Service,' he added grandly, for he always liked to make the grand gesture when he dared.

The tall, dark-haired youth was impressed. He stared up at the swarthy agent with his hooked nose, obviously intrigued. 'Ah, the famed English Secret Service,' he said with a gravity beyond his years. 'Please enter.'

Sidney Reilly followed him into the little, sparsely furnished room, heated by a green-tiled oven which reached to the ceiling and on which lay an old woman with a shawl wrapped around her head. Reilly saw immediately that she was dying.

'*Babuska*,' the boy said simply. 'She saved me and has hidden me from those Red beasts for the last six years.'

On the stone oven bench, the old woman moaned.

'Now the poor dear's time has about come.' There were tears in the boy's eyes. 'Friends of the old court brought us to this strange place once they heard *Babuska* could look after me no longer. They said the Englishman would see to everything. So what will you do?'

Now it was Reilly's turn to be impressed. Although the boy had been living among peasants ever since the Romanov family had been murdered, he still retained the aristocratic directness of his dead father, the Tsar.

'I have been commanded by your uncle King George V *personally*,' Reilly lied, 'to bring you out of Russia and transport you secretly to Great Britain.'

'How?' the boy asked directly.

'It is better, Your Highness, that you don't know the details of our plan. There is some danger entailed. If you are caught by the police, you will know nothing. You will be just more of the Homeless Ones.' Reilly meant the thousands of children orphaned during the Civil War who wandered around Russia trying to steal a living and dodge the police.

'I understand.' The boy accepted the information without any further comment. 'But what about *Babuska*? I can't leave till she has finally passed away.' Again, tears flooded his bright blue eyes.

'We shall wait,' Reilly agreed. 'Perhaps you will give me a cup of water from over there?' He indicated the white pail covered with a towel. 'We'll make her drink a little. It might bring her round for a moment and then I can see what her condition's like.'

The boy turned and took the mug down from the nail above the bucket. While his back was so turned, Reilly palmed the pill he had brought with him specifically for this purpose. Those friends of the old Court who had brought the pair to this strange hiding place had told him – these days in Russia everyone became very talkative at the first sight of a Horseman of St George – that the boy would never leave without the old woman.

Reilly took the mug, dropped the pill into it, and then, wrinkling his nose a little at the unwashed stench coming from the dying peasant woman, fed her a little water. Most of it went down her wrinkled, shaking chin but the pill went down her throat. He made sure of that, raising her skinny back a little so that she swallowed it. 'It's no use,' he said in mock sadness, as he gently lowered her once more. 'She's in a deep coma. I'm afraid the inevitable won't be very long now. Then we shall start our journey.'

'But who will bury her?' the boy protested, his haughty aristocratic mien vanished now. 'Who will ensure that she is buried in her native earth?' He reached in his pocket to pull out a little leather bag. He opened the drawstrings and showed Reilly the dark earth inside it. Obviously, Reilly told himself, the woman was of Cossack stock. They always carried the earth from their native Don with them so that they could be buried in their own soil.

'The woman who owns this place will see to it, Your Highness. I shall pay her one Horseman of St George.' He pulled a gold sovereign from his pocket to show the boy what he meant. Behind him the old woman was beginning to moan and move. The cyanide pill was already taking effect.

The boy turned in alarm. He placed his

hand, which Reilly noted with approval was unkept and hardened like that of a peasant boy, on the dying woman's face and stroked it gently.

He feigned concern as little flecks of foam started to form at the side of her lips, which were already blue. Reilly told himself she had only moments to live. It would be dark outside now. It would provide them with the cover they needed to dodge the police patrols which were everywhere now that Lenin lay dying in the Kremlin. Obviously the authorities feared trouble soon.

Suddenly the old woman arched her back, her ancient wrinkled face contorted by unbearable pain. She opened her eyes. She saw Reilly's dark face peering over the shoulder of her beloved boy. 'Serge' – she faltered so weakly that the Grand Duke had to bend his head to hear – 'Serge … beware of...' Her hand like a shrunken claw raised itself slowly and came to a rest, pointing at Reilly. 'Beware,' she began again, her voice even more feeble, 'of that–' Abruptly she fell backwards onto the stone pillow. She was dead.

The boy fought to control himself, his lips quivering as he forced himself to be brave and not cry. With apparent gentleness, Reilly took him by the shoulders and led him towards the door. He then returned and closed the old crone's eyes. 'It is time to go, Your Highness,' he said, his voice hushed with reverence.

The boy took one last look at the old peasant woman who had saved his life. 'Goodbye, *Babuska*,' he said thickly, still fighting back the tears, 'I will never forget you.' He crossed himself and then allowed himself to be led down that dark and dangerous tunnel which ran to Madame Discretion's rooms.

Inside the *salon*, they were preparing for the night's trade. A woman, naked but for black silk stockings, was squatting over a bucket of warm water, washing her hairy crotch. Others were soaking little bits of sponge in vinegar. They would be shoved into their vaginas to provide a primitive form of contraceptive. Others were slipping into black and red silk knickers and then applying rouge to their nipples. All was hectic activity, punctuated by bursts of raucous laughter and quick puffs at long cigarettes which festooned the ashtrays everywhere. Reilly looked from the whores to the boy. He seemed to be taking it in his stride, as if he went into brothels every day of his life.

The two of them crossed over to where Madame Discretion, well corseted now and clad in black silk, sat behind the desk waiting to receive her clients – and take their money. 'That old woman is dead. You'll see she gets a decent burial.'

'And don't forget to sprinkle her native earth over her,' the boy said.

Reilly winked at the fat brothel owner. She looked at him knowingly. The old woman would be tossed into the sewer and washed away into the Moskva River. Reilly never left any traces behind. In his business it was not wise to.

Madame Discretion looked at the boy, for the first time curious. Who was he? she wondered. What was so important about him that his friends and the Jew were prepared to pay a small fortune to hide him? 'Where you go?' she asked in broken Russian.

'*Ça suffit*,' Reilly cut in hurriedly in case the boy answered. He held out his hand. 'Goodbye, madame and thank you.' He put on his hat and holding the boy's hand firmly in his own stepped out into the night. A moment later they had vanished down the street.

Chapter Two

The Cheka raided Madame Discretion's two hours later. Brothels were outlawed in the new Soviet State but they were tolerated by the Secret Police, especially if the owner, as did Madame Discretion, greased their palms well enough. Unfortunately for the fat Frenchwoman one of her 'girls' had transmitted syphilis to the secretary of Josef Stalin. The secretary had been forced to confess the reason for his illness to 'old leatherface', as Stalin was called behind his back. Stalin had flown into a terrible rage and had ordered Madame Discretion's closed down at once.

Now, as Reilly and Serge were setting off on their long journey to freedom, the Chekists forced their way through the door of the brothel, past Madame Discretion's two bouncers and into the 'establishment', as the fat Frenchwoman liked to call her place, itself. Screaming girls, mostly naked, were thrown out of their rooms. A future marshal of the Soviet Union was found tied up in chains to a wall. A fat commissar was discovered in bed with two of Madame Discretion's youngest whores, dressed as prerevolutionary schoolgirls, who protested when he was arrested, 'I was must making a survey, comrades, for the Five Year Plan! Just a survey!'

It was about the time that the fat commissar and his two 'schoolgirls' were arrested that the Chekists penetrated into the tunnel and discovered the secret room at its end. They were not particularly surprised by the tunnel and the secret room; old Moscow was riddled with such places, said to date back to the days of the mad Tsar, Ivan the Terrible. But it was the old woman dead on the oven bench which took them by surprise. What, they asked, was an obviously peasant woman doing hiding below a brothel? Why, too, was she carrying a picture of the dead Romanovs in her shabby bag?

The commissar in charge of the raiding party, a big one-eyed ex-sailor who had gained his position because he had been a member of the crew of the cruiser *Aurora,* which had started the revolution back in '17, was not particularly bright. But he did realise all the same that there was something strange here.

'Bring the fat Frog whore-mother to me,' he ordered his Chekists, who were already half-drunk from the place's vodka which they had looted.

Moments later they had dragged her in. Her dress was ripped, to reveal her massive breasts, and her wig had slipped to one side to show that she was almost bald beneath it. Yet she was still defiant, cursing in French *'Sales cons russes'* and threatening in broken Russian, 'I make you pay for this.'

'Shut up, whore-mother!' the one-eyed policeman growled and routinely slapped the Frenchwoman cross her fat, powdered face. 'What's that old woman doing dead in your secret room?' he asked. 'Come on, spit it out. *Davoi.*'

'I spit in your mother's milk!' she shrieked, eyes blazing with anger. 'You'll pay for this—' She stopped suddenly as he hit her again, but harder this time. She stared at him, shocked. No one had hit her like that since her days in Marseilles where her pimp had taken great pleasure in beating her up when he was drunk, which was most of the time.

'Well?' he demanded, lighting one of the cigarettes he had looted, savouring the rich foreign tobacco which made a nice change from the coarse black Russian stuff smoked through a roll of old newspaper.

'Friends brought them,' she said reluctantly. 'They paid me to hide them down there.' She tugged at her torn dress, trying to hide her breasts. 'That's all.'

He took his time, knowing, as stupid as he was, that he was on to something. 'Why?' he asked.

'I don't know. In my business you don't ask. You give what the client wants.'

'Yes,' he said, thinking of Stalin's diseased secretary, 'like a dose of clap, for example.' He laughed at his own humour then was serious again. 'But you said *them*, whore. Where's the other one?'

'He went with the man,' she said dully, realising that she had got herself into a mess now. She ought to have asked more questions right at the outset.

The Cheka officer pushed back his peaked cap and scratched the front of his shaven skull. Things were getting complicated, he told himself. But there might be something in this one for him. 'What man?'

'I don't know,' she said. 'Just a man. He gave me money and took the boy away with him.'

Almost routinely he took the fine foreign cigarette from his mouth, blew on the glowing end and then applied it to her naked left breast just above the nipple.

She screamed and reeled back, holding her massive dug in both hands, sudden tears of pain streaming down her fat cheeks, making trails through the powder.

'Now then, no more farting about, or you'll have more of that. You'd better start talking – and talking fast.' The Cheka stared at her grimly. 'Now then, whore, get on with it...'

Aronson received the news just before midnight. He was lying on the couch in his office, reading. Ever since his days as a subversive, he had made it his habit to change his place of rest every night. Sometimes he slept at the home of his wife, more often at the homes of his mistresses. Now and again he slept on the couch in his office. He had known well the ways of *Okhrana,* the Imperial Secret Police. They had always come to arrest their victims at night. It had been wise to keep changing one's sleeping quarters. Now the habit had persisted even though he was the one who did the arresting these days.

He was lying there half-dressed, rereading Tolstoy's *War and Peace* and repeatedly telling himself that that was the real, heroic, undying Russia that he had always loved, when Ilona knocked and came in. She was on night duty; otherwise he would have slept with her this night.

'What news, comrade?' he asked, formally till she closed the door. 'The Soviet State never sleeps.' He winked and she winked back.

She crossed over to where he lay and sat down at the edge of the couch before handing him the message. 'From the Moscow Cheka,' she said and ran her hand over his bare hairy chest lovingly. 'Very strange. But I thought it might have some remote connection with what that woman had to say about the Romanovs. You know the one, who com–'

'–I know,' he said and gently pushed away her importuning hand, which had now descended to his stomach. 'You are a very intelligent but naughty woman, Ilona, you know. Here, let me see.' Swiftly, while she waited, he read through the arrest report taken from some Cheka officer named Smirnov. His agent in the Moscow Cheka always signalled such things if he thought they might interest Aronson.

He sucked his front teeth thoughtfully after he had finished it. Thinking aloud, he said slowly, 'A handsome, well-spoken boy

113

in the charge of an old dying peasant woman... A stranger who comes to fetch the boy and tips the madam of the brothel in English sovereigns ... a Jew by the looks of him who speaks French and Russian and Yiddish as well. Hm...' Again Aronson sniffed and once again Ilona laid her hand gently on his bare chest. Aronson did not seem to notice. He was too deep in thought.

'Reilly,' he said suddenly and she jumped.

He sat up. 'Reilly. The man has to be Reilly. Speaking those languages and looking Jewish. More importantly, he paid the brothel owner in the Horsemen of St George.'

She looked at his flushed, excited face in bewilderment. 'Reilly ... I don't understand.'

Swiftly he explained to her who Reilly was. Then he said, 'It has to be him. All his career, Reilly has been more than just a spy. He was never content to be just a cog in the wheel of intelligence and espionage. He has always taken delight in shaping policy himself and acquiring power. What better time to try to follow that Napoleonic urge of his – he admires Napoleon and collects relics of the French emperor – than now with the Soviet state in flux. Anything – everything – could happen and that cunning fiend Reilly would,

I'm sure, dearly love to make things happen.'

She was still bewildered. 'But what can one man do, darling?' she asked. 'One man against all those powerful people in Moscow?'

'You underestimate him, Ilona,' Aronson answered. 'He is the man who almost convinced the English government to start a counter-revolution against the Soviets six years ago. He certainly was the brain behind the Anglo-French-American intervention in our affairs that same year.' He stopped and his handsome face wrinkled in a frown. 'Let us just suppose,' he said after a few moments, 'that there is an unknown heir to the Romanov throne and Reilly has got his paws on to him – perhaps that boy who was with the old woman in Moscow – what would he do with him? To what purpose would he use the Romanov?'

Ilona's dark green eyes glowed suddenly at his words. Aronson knew why. At heart his mistress and office spy was a monarchist. Ever since her father, the Admiral, had been murdered by his own sailors not more than two versts from where they were now, she had hated the 'Reds', as she called them privately to him. 'To restore the Imperial throne,' she said eagerly. 'Then we could all be happy once more.'

He looked at her. 'Happy? Were the millions of serfs happy?' he asked, then dropped the matter. 'You're perhaps right, Ilona. That could well be his dream. Like his hero Napoleon he would have created a king. After all, Napoleon must have created at least three of them. What a sense of power that would give our Mister Reilly.' He leaned back on the couch, hands behind his head. 'But of course, this is all conjecture, Ilona—' He stopped short.

'But *this* isn't, is it, dearest?' she simpered, as she slid her hand on to his crotch.

He laughed softly. 'You really are a naughty girl, Ilona.'

She didn't answer. She couldn't. Aronson sighed. Then he lay back with her head on his lap and let himself enjoy it.

Chapter Three

A thin grey mist hung over the Baltic. It clung to the rocks along the coast so that they looked like bearded giants. A mysterious stillness brooded over the still sea as the little

Swedish steamer chugged eastwards at a steady ten knots an hour. Standing on the rusting deck, muffled up to the eyes, Billy Bennett was chewing at a piece of cold fried bread in between snatches of the old wartime ditty, *'Don't cryee … don't sighee … there's a silver lining in the skyee… Cheerio, chin-chin, napoo … tootle-oo…Wipe the tear, baby dear, from your eyee… Goodbyee…'*

'Put a sock in it, Billy,' his shipmate Ginger Kerrigan said. 'You and yer bloody goodbye!' He shivered and slapped his arms about his skinny body. 'Ruddy brass monkey weather today.'

'Only trying to cheer mesen up,' Billy Bennett said, taking a last bite at the cold fried bread. 'With the kind o' bleeding grub them Swedes serve – all that raw fish rubbish – a bloke needs cheering up, don't 'e?'

Ginger Kerrigan pulled the dewdrop off the end of his long red nose and slung it expertly over the side. They were a day and a half out of Hull now and passing through the straits that led into the Baltic proper. As far as he could see, the inland sea was empty. Indeed, they hadn't sighted a vessel since the day before. But then, Ginger told himself, it was a Sunday, and a freezing January Sunday to boot. Merchant seamen hated to be sailing at a weekend. That was the time when they were snug in some pub or knocking-shop, making up for a long boring week at sea. He sighed. At this particular moment on a freezing morning like this, he wouldn't have said no to a pint of wallop and a warm tart.

Up on the bridge, taking their morning exercise, Bird and Smith were pretty much of the same mood. Their breakfast had been served them by a pretty blonde Swedish stewardess but she was as bland and as boring as the food. Now Dickie Bird sighed and said, 'When we get to port, old bean, I'm going to go the whole *totus porcus* – the whole hog.'

Now it was Smith's turn to sigh and say, 'Dickie, I wish you wouldn't go in for that awful public schoolboy slang. Should have left that behind you when we departed Harrow-on-the-Hill.'

Dickie didn't seem to hear Smith's objection. 'I'm going to get myself some decent scoff, a pint of champers and a nice keen young filly–' He broke off suddenly.

'What is it?' Smith asked hastily.

'To port,' Dickie answered. 'Visitors.'

Smith acted immediately. 'All right you lot,' he called to Ginger Kerrigan and Bennett, 'get out of sight.' He nodded to the grizzled Swedish captain with a cigar clenched in the side of his mouth and the bottle of aquavit in the pocket of his shabby jacket. 'You see to them, skipper?'

The Swede shifted the cigar from one side of his mouth to the other and growled, *'Ja, I do.'*

Now, sheltering in the lee of the bridge, the two Englishmen watched as the small craft, painted a light blue, came slowly out of the fog, a man mounting the searchlight on the superstructure while another couple waited next to the quick-firer. 'Looks like one of those damned Hun sub-chasers which the Huns used to run out of Zeebrugge during the last show,' Dickie Bird said.

Smith nodded his agreement. 'Yes, very definitely, and she's coming our way.' He strained his eyes and read the white-painted legend on the other craft's side. *'Wasser ... schutz ... polizei...'* he said slowly. 'That's the Hun water police.'

'So it is,' Dickie retorted, 'but aren't they a bit out of German territorial waters?' he added.

'You're right. They definitely are.' Smith pressed himself closer into the shadows, as the fast patrol boat started to slow down and draw alongside the ancient coal-burning Swedish freighter. A German in police uniform came out of the bridge with a loud-hailer. In German he asked, 'What's your cargo? Where are you bound?'

The Swedish skipper told him in broken, heavily accented German as the two young British officers waited tensely. They knew that the Germans had no right to stop another vessel outside German territorial waters. But they could hardly object, especially with those two tough-looking policemen standing next to the quick-firer. Both of them knew their Germans of old. As Dickie Bird was often wont to say, 'Wouldn't trust a deuced Hun as far as I could throw him. Beastly race!'

The man on the bridge of the German vessel stared hard at the little freighter with its rusting superstructure and its unpainted plates. 'What's in those crates?' he asked after a few moments.

The Swedish skipper knew well enough what was in them – the *Swordfish*. But he feigned innocence with all the authority of a professional actor. He pushed his battered cap to the back of his head, scratched his hair, pulled his nose and said finally, 'Well, I don't rightly know. The agent said machinery. And that's what it reads on the manifest. So that's what they'll be, eh?'

The German stared up at him in disgust, as if he were dealing with an idiot. 'A captain should know every item of his cargo intimately,' he warned.

The old skipper chuckled. 'The only thing I know intimately, German, is my old woman ... and I don't know her that intimately these days.' He chuckled again and fumbled with his flies to make his meaning quite clear.

The German shook his head and then he said, catching the skipper by surprise, 'And where are you from?'

Without thinking the Swede answered, 'Hull' in the very same instant that Billy Bennett slipped on the icy deck as he tried to get below and cried out at the top of his voice, 'Bloody hell, knocked me right off me plates o' meat!'

Smith knew at once that the German had heard. He could see it in the policeman's hard face. He knew, too, that the cop would already be asking himself, what was an Englishman doing aboard a rundown old Swedish freighter?

But the German did not react. Instead he touched his hand to his cap in salute and called to the Swede, *'Schon gut, Herr Kapitan. Gute Fahrt,'* before returning inside the bridge. Moments later the vessel was underway once more, disappearing into the thin mist, her engines roaring as the craft put on speed.

Bird and Smith came out of their hiding place and stared in the direction the German craft had taken. But already she had disappeared.

'The Hun spotted us,' Smith said pensively. 'The crates, that Hull and that damned fool Bennett shouting in English were a dead giveaway.'

'I'm afraid so, old chap,' Dickie agreed. 'Still, he said ta-ta politely enough and tootled off nicely, didn't he?'

'Yes,' Smith answered, face suddenly worried, 'but is he going to stay away? Will his friends soon make an appearance?'

'In the lap of the Gods, old thing,' Dickie said airily. 'Kismet and all that, what?'

But Smith wasn't leaving it to chance. He strode over to the elderly skipper, who was again 'refreshing' himself, as he called it, from his flat bottle of spirits and asked him to alter course immediately. They would sail close to the Swedish coast now till they reached a point below Sundsvall where they would steer directly eastwards for Finland. And they would keep within Swedish territorial waters. It would be safer that way. 'The Germans wouldn't dare enter Swedish waters, skipper.'

The old Swede, faded old eyes glowing again with the effect of the strong spirit, chuckled thickly and said, 'You don't know the German gentlemen, Mr Smith. In my time I have seen a lot of them. The German, he do what he likes.' He chuckled again and then concentrated on bringing the ship about.

Time passed leadenly. In their tiny and dirty little cabin, Smith and Bird read while in the fo'c'sle, the crew of the *Swordfish* did the same or played cards, while CPO Ferguson watched the players, that old Calvinist stern look on his withered face, murmuring at periodical intervals, 'Yon's a mug's game. Ye'll allus find there's one o' you card sharpers in every game.' A comment frowned upon by Ginger Kerrigan, who happened to have an extra ace concealed in the sleeve of his jersey. 'What's it matter, Chiefie?' he retorted, 'we're only playing for tabs.' He indicated the heap of cigarette ends resting in his cap in the middle of the players.

But the old chief petty officer wasn't convinced. 'It's the way o' the dee-vil,' he announced. 'Not a farthing o' good can come of it.' Then he lapsed into a moody silence.

Outside the light was going early, as it always did in these northern regions and on the bridge, the old captain, already half-drunk on the aquavit, was slow to see the two biplanes emerging from the darkening sky. Routinely he raised his glasses, as he had always done during the war when he had heard the sound of aircraft engines. Neutral Swedish as his ship had been, he had always found it safer to turn on all the vessel's lights so that the pilots recognized her for what she was.

Two Fokker biplanes slid into the circles of calibrated glass. The one was painted bright red, as if it might belong to some flying circus, of which there were many touring the Baltic countries during the summer. The other was painted blue, a sky blue which would merge with the sky on a normal day. But both did not seem to bear any badges of identification.

He frowned. 'They're probably Swedish,' he said to himself in the manner of all lonely men. 'After all, they are coming from the Swedish mainland.' Still he couldn't overcome the feeling that there was something strange about the two Fokkers. Where were they going at this time of the day with the light already going? Normally pilots didn't fly in the hours of darkness, especially civilian ones. They didn't have the instruments to do so.

Suddenly the pilot of the red plane waggled his wings. It was a signal to the other one. Its pilot, too, waggled his wings, as if in answer. The planes started to come down lower. Now he could just make out the dark shapes of the pilots' heads in their leather helmets in their open cockpits. Abruptly he gasped. Both planes, although they didn't bear the markings of the Swedish Royal Air Force, were armed with machine guns. He could see the two machine guns fastened to the engine cowling quite clearly now. He grabbed for the speaking tube, pulled out the plug and whistled sharply.

Down below, Smith reached for his end. He pulled out the plug. 'What is it, skipper?' he asked casually.

'There's something strange here, mister,' the Swede answered. 'Aeroplanes bearing down on us. Better come up topside and have a look.'

Smith sprang out of his bunk and peered through the dirty porthole. He caught a glimpse of a Fokker biplane coming in very low. Then another, painted a bright shining red.

'Two planes!' he cried. 'One of them red.'

'*Red!*' Dickie shouted above the roar of the engines. 'Let me have a dekko!'

He pushed Smith to one side. The latter hurriedly put on his boots while Dickie Bird peered out of the porthole. Suddenly he gave out a low whistle. 'You know, Smithie, who always painted his plane red during the last show so that our chaps would know exactly who they were tangling with?'

Smith, busy with his bootlaces, shook his head.

'I'll tell you then – *the Red Baron!*'

'Who?'

'You know, you soft-headed mutt, Baron von Richthofen.'

'Oh crikey. Let's get up topside p.d.q.'

'Pretty Damned Quick it is,' Dickie Bird echoed and then they were running up the companionway as fast as their legs could carry them.

Chapter Four

Goering felt a pleasant tingling throughout his fat body, allied to a growing sense of excitement. This, he told himself, was like in the old days when they'd be up above the trenches waiting to pounce upon some unsuspecting Tommy or Frog; then falling out of the sky, twin machine guns chattering.

He poked his gloved hand above the cockpit and pointed downwards. Hartmann responded. He had understood. He would go in first. Goering would follow.

Hartmann pushed the stick forward. The Fokker's nose tilted. Hartmann fell out of the sky. Goering watched. *'Four hundred metres … three hundred … two hundred and fifty…'*

'Come on, man!' he urged. 'Do it now or you'll be in the shitting drink!'

Even as he yelled his warning, Hartmann tugged at the stick. The Fokkers shuddered violently. Next moment Hartmann opened fire. The slugs flew towards the battered old freighter. Tracer belted along the whole superstructure. A mast went down. Angry blue sparks rose from the live wires as they touched the rusty deck. Then Hartmann was zooming away up into the grey misty sky once again and Goering knew it was his turn.

He sucked his bottom lip, said a quick prayer, then pushed the stick forward. The freighter was a sitting duck, he knew. She had no means of defending herself as far as he could see. But he couldn't knock her out with 9mm machine-gun bullet. He had to puncture something vital, set her on fire. Now, as he screamed out of the sky, his flabby flesh pushed against the bones of his broad face by the air pressure, he aimed for the boiler room, ignoring the men running towards the two large crates which the *Wasserschutzpolizei* had reported being on the deck. *Three hundred ... two hundred and fifty metres...* His eyes flew from his target to the altimeter and back again... *Two hundred metres ... one fifty metres...*

'Enough!' he commanded himself. Next instant his finger pressed the firing button. Suddenly the cockpit was full of the acrid stench of burned cordite as the machine guns strapped to the Fokker's nose burst into frantic activity. Red tracer flew towards the freighter like a flight of angry hornets. On deck a sailor threw up his arms in a melo-

dramatic fashion and remained thus for what seemed a long time before his knees gave beneath him and he crumpled to the deck. Smoke started to pour from somewhere. Next moment Goering had levelled out and was skimming across the ship at mast height.

Down below Smith cursed. Next to him, Dickie Bird yelled above the racket the Fokker's racing engines made, 'I'd give a lot to put a burst up those Hun swines' rumps!'

'Break out the rifles,' Smith cried, desperately, 'we've got to do something.'

'Ye heard the officer!' CPO Ferguson bellowed. 'Away with ye and get ye rifles!'

'But we're neutral,' the Swedish skipper protested as the crew of the *Swordfish* scattered.

'Frigging well tell that to *them!*' Ginger Kerrigan panted as he ran to fetch his weapon.

Goering circled round in a tight turn. A hundred metres or so off, Hartmann was in the lead, already preparing for a second attack. Goering nodded his approval and looked down at the ship. Thick black smoke was pouring from her hull. But at present there was no sign of fire, though she was beginning to list a little. He licked suddenly dry lips and told himself they would have to finish her off this time. Soon it would be completely dark and they had a fifty-kilometre flight in front of them back to their Swedish coastal base. Hartmann flung a glance over his shoulder. Goering raised his gloved hand: the signal for attack. Hartmann nodded. Next moment he flung his Fokker out of the sky, motor racing, heading in for the second and final attack.

Watching him go in, Goering felt that old excitement. This was what life was about – a fight between life and death. *'Hals und Beinbuch, Hans!'* he yelled though he knew it was impossible for Hartmann to hear him.

Now Hartmann had levelled out about two hundred metres from the freighter. This time he would go in at virtually sea-level, flying just above stalling speed to make sure that his bullets would 'sit', as they had said in the war. Goering nodded his approval. That was the way to do it, especially as the freighter was not armed. At the speed Hartmann was flying now, he would be a sitting duck otherwise.

On the deck of the freighter, his nostrils already assailed by the smell of something burning, Smith cried, 'Give him a concentrated volley when I command fire. We just might get lucky.'

'Ay,' Ginger Kerrigan muttered *sotto voce,*

'and frigging pigs might fly.' All the same he squinted through his sight, lining up the plane which approached at what seemed a very slow speed.

Smith tensed. The plane was coming closer. Dare he hold his fire much longer? He told himself he must. With the freighter already beginning to list, the crew of the *Swordfish* would find it difficult enough to aim accurately.

Now, despite the mist, Smith could see the plane and its pilot quite clearly: a black-masked, begoggled Hun, for he was sure their attackers were German, sat tensed over his controls, finger probably poised over his firing button. In a second or two, he'd press it and then once again all hell would be let loose.

Smith raised his revolver. He knew it was like swotting an elephant with a peashooter. But it was better than nothing. Otherwise he would have felt absolutely helpless. 'Stand by everybody!' he yelled above the roar of the Fokker's racing engine.

They raised their rifles, tucking them into their right shoulders, squinting along the sights. On the plane, Hartmann pressed his button. In front of him the twin air-cooled machine guns burst into crazy life. Tracer zipped lethally towards the old freighter. Angry sparks erupted along the side of her metal hide. A lifeboat splintered into matchwood. Another's lines were severed and tumbled into the mirrorlike sea.

'*Fire!*' Smith yelled desperately, as the plane roared towards them, twin machine guns blazing.

They needed no urging. As one they pressed their triggers. Slugs sailed through the air. The Fokker was almost on to them now, it seemed to fill the whole darkening sky. Nothing could stop it. Hartmann's face contorted into a triumphant snarl behind the mask. He'd sink the bastard this time.

Suddenly, startlingly, the little shield in front of him cracked into a crazy spider's web. He yelled in abrupt agony. In an instant he was blinded, blood jetting in scarlet profusion from his right. '*Nein!*' he screamed, high and hysterical like a woman. '*Nein bitte!*'

Panic-stricken and shocked, seeing nothing but a red veil in front of his eyes, he tried to fly on, hands gripping the joystick in white-knuckled fear.

Down below, Ginger Kerrigan cried out in alarm, 'Christ, the silly git's coming straight for us!'

132

Smith saw the Liverpudlian was right. Smoke from the plane's shattered engine must be blinding the pilot, he told himself in sudden alarm as the Fokker headed straight for the freighter. *'Duck!'* he shrieked. *'Duck everybo–'*

His cry of alarm was drowned by the great rending and tearing of tortured metal as the Fokker slammed straight into the ship not far from the hull. The freighter reeled alarmingly. One of her masts touched the water for a moment. Down below they could hear the cries of fear and panic as the off-duty crew members were thrown out of their bunks.

'Holy cow!' Dickie Bird yelled. 'We've taken a packet this ruddy time!'

They had. The freighter was listing badly to port and even as the second plane came racing into the attack, Smith could hear the water gurgling and belching obscenely as the sea poured through the ruptured plates. Up on the bridge, the skipper sounded the alarm bells and ducked as the glass in front of him shattered, machine-gun bullets slamming into the metal like heavy summer rain on a tin roof. Then Goering's plane was sailing up into the dark sky, trailing smoke behind it. A minute later it had vanished into the darkness, heading for home base.

Now all was darkness. Slowly the heavily listed freighter limped towards the coast. Below, the wounded and burned were being tended to, their wounds bandaged with rags and teacloths, while the cook was rubbing butter on the burns of those who had been scalded when one of the boilers had burst.

Up on deck, Dickie Bird and an anxious Smith surveyed the two enormous crates which contained the two halves of the *Swordfish* with their torches. They had been hit, that was clear. There were bulletholes ripped in the wood the length of both crates. 'The question is whether those damned bullets hit anything vital on the *Swordfish*,' Smith expressed his fears aloud.

'Well, they say the proof of the pudding is in the eating, Smithie,' Dickie answered. 'And that we'll only know when we reach Sweden.' He corrected himself as the battered freighter with her buckled plates gave another frightening shudder. '*If* we reach Sweden.'

Smith nodded grimly and stared through the cold night darkness, as if willing the land to appear. But the Swedish coast remained obstinately out of sight. He couldn't even spot the light of a lighthouse which the old skipper had told him was in this area some-where. 'What do you think, Dickie?' He broke the heavy silence. 'If the worse came to the worse, do you think those two crates would float?'

Dickie Bird looked at him puzzled in the light of his torch. Then it dawned on him which direction his old shipmate's thoughts were going. 'I get you. If this old tub goes down before we reach shore, would they float by themselves?' He grunted and thought for a few seconds. 'They have been holed with those Hun's bullets, of course, and in the second crate the *Swordfish's* engine room is wide open. That crate would go down like a brick if the water got inside that. But my guess is, old bean, that with the sea as calm as this, we might just get away with it, if we have to ditch the crates.'

'My thinking exactly,' Smith said, reassured as the freighter gave yet another shudder and a 'chippy' came running up hastily with his tools, ready to caulk yet another ruptured plate.

'What's the drill then?'

'This. Get the chaps up on deck with as many warm togs on as they can find.'

'Then?'

'We cut the restraining lines, Dickie. If this

old tub goes down we float' – he crossed his fingers behind his back at the words – 'once this deck is below the surface. With a bit of luck we can then reach the coast and see what we can do about getting the old *Swordfish* in one piece again. Or somehow continue with the original plan of getting her into position by rail.'

'There's a deuced lot of jolly old ifs,' Dickie Bird said in that languid manner of his. 'But I 'spect we'll be able to pull it off, as the actress said to the bishop.' He chuckled at his own humour. 'I'll go and rouse the chaps.'

'Good. Just one more thing, Dickie.'

'What's that, old sport?'

'See that the men are armed at all times now,' Smith replied, his voice very serious. 'It's obvious that the Huns are on to us. It won't take the Russkis long to do the same, is my guess. We can't take any more chances. We must be on our guard all the time now. All right, cut along, old chap, that's it.'

Smith turned and stared hard into the glowing silver darkness over the Baltic, as if he could see enemies everywhere…

Chapter Five

The British Consul tugged his long nose and said somewhat ponderously, 'How could it happen, you ask? How could obviously Hun planes from the last show attack you from Swedish territory? I shall tell you.' He stared hard at the two young men in their salt-stained civilian clothes.

'In this year of 1924 *anything* can happen. Europe and the Near East are in total disarray. The old empires, the German, the Russian, the Turkish, have disappeared. With them the certainties of politics have vanished, too. In their place we've got lots of little states. Look at the Baltic seaboard alone: we've got *four* new national states. Here race fights race and religion fights religion or creed.' He sighed like a sorely tried man and mopped his brow with a big flowered silk handkerchief. 'None of the surviving great powers are prepared to do anything about the situation. Even if we, the British, have to do what we can, unofficially. So what do countries like Sweden do? I'll tell you. They turn a blind eye to things, especially if by doing something they might endanger their trade with Germany.' He looked through the window of his office at the snow falling outside in a solid white sheet, as if the snowstorm was yet another burden he was forced to bear, and sighed. 'I expect the old Empire will come through in the end. But it's all very difficult, very, very difficult.'

The freighter had finally gone down half a mile out of Malmö, the port at the most southerly tip of Sweden. With a violent lurch which had nearly thrown the shivering frozen crew of the *Swordfish* from their perch on the two bullet-holed crates, the ship had started to take in even more water. For a few minutes Smith had feared the freighter might well keel over, but luckily for them and their precious crates it hadn't. Instead it had gone down fairly evenly and the crates had simply floated away, while all around the Swedes had threshed the freezing water frantically in their attempts to get into the lifeboats before they froze to death.

In the pitch darkness it had been difficult to steer the unwieldy crates using boat hooks as oars. But once they had spotted the lights of Malmö harbour, it had been easier. At two in the morning, chilled to the bone, and exhausted from the back-breaking work of keeping the crates going in the right direction, they had landed on the strand just outside the harbour, where they had managed to light fires from driftwood and warm themselves. 'Heaven help a frigging sailor on a night like this,' Ginger Kerrigan had proclaimed as he had held his frozen, chapped palms up to the first flames of the fire. 'Why didn't I join the frigging brown jobs?' He meant the army. It was a sentiment with which they had all heartily agreed.

At first light Smith had ventured into the port and with the aid of those much sought after 'Horsemen of St George', he managed to get one of the many stallholders, who catered for the local seamen to sell him two large thermos flasks filled with hot water and tea, plus a generous portion of rum. '*Teepunsch*,' the stall owner had chortled happily after pocketing the sovereign. 'Very good … very good.'

It was indeed. It had put new heart in the men. Their spirits had risen immediately. Now, full of *teepunsch* and the ham rolls which Smith had bought later, they were sheltering in a makeshift lean-to between the crates, while Smith and Bird reported to the Consul.

The Consul, who also acted as the local passport control officer, which was the usual cover for one of C's agents abroad, had already reported their whereabouts to Queen Anne's Gate. Now he commenced their briefing. 'I have already made arrangements for halftracks–'

'–Halftracks, sir?' Smith broke in almost immediately. 'What are those?'

The Consul said, 'In the kind of winters we get out here, nothing but tracked vehicles can move on the roads. So the Swedes have lorries, which are wheeled *and* tracked – only way to get about in this damned snow.' He sighed yet again. 'What I wouldn't give to be on some desert island at this moment, surrounded by dusky maidens! God, all that damned snow. No wonder the Swedes are always killing themselves. Where was I, now?'

'You're providing us with these – er – halftracks,' Smith prompted.

'Oh, yes. They'll get you across the country to Sundsvall. There you'll find a coastal freighter waiting to take you across to Finland. The sooner you're out of this damned country the better. The Finns are, on the whole, pro-British. At all events since they freed themselves from the Russians, they've been anti-Russian. You'll be safer there.'

Smith nodded his understanding and asked, 'What about the drivers of the half-tracks?'

'My own people,' the Consul replied promptly. 'Jose and Pedro – brought them back with me as servants when I was posted here from Portuguese Africa. Most reliable.'

'Do you mean, sir, they're darkies?' Dickie Bird asked, a little surprised.

'Of course, black as the ace of spades. But utterly loyal. Wish some of our own people in Africa and India were that loyal. Trust 'em with my life.'

Smith shot Dickie a glance and knew he was thinking the same. God knows what Chiefie Ferguson's reaction was going to be. 'Do they speak the lingo?' he asked the Consul.

'Yes, some. Enough at least to get whatever you may need till you get to your destination.' He lowered his voice. 'Just one more thing.'

'Sir?'

'At Sundsvall, you'll be joined by someone important, namely,' he lowered his voice even further, 'the wife of Sidney Reilly. She knows his plan. She'll give you further instructions.'

'Have you met her, sir?' Smith asked quickly.

'Yes, I have. She is a very beautiful woman indeed. A swell dish, as they used to say when I was in the States.' He smiled for the first time since they had met him, as if at some fond memory. 'But a dangerous woman. Can't put my finger on it exactly.' The Consul pursed his lips. 'But dangerous ... just like her husband, I suppose. All right then, I'll ring for Jose and Pedro.'

'*Darkies!*' CPO Ferguson snorted with disgust, as the two huge half-tracked trucks churned to a stop. 'I'll ha' nae truck with yon black fellers.'

'Don't talk so loud, Chiefie,' Dickie said with a grin, although the snow was pelting down in a white fury. 'They might get offended. They're probably cannibals.'

Jose and Pedro, muffled up in cheap furs, grinned from behind the wheels of their heated cabs.

'I dinna like it,' Ferguson persisted. 'Nae good of it. Darkies!' he snorted once more and then he stamped away to where the crew were preparing the first crate for loading.

Smith looked at the sky, heavy with snow, and said, 'Thank God for those tracks. This little lot looks as if it's going to continue all day.'

'Yes,' Dickie agreed. 'All the same, it'll give us the cover we need. Remember what his nibs the Consul said, "Don't trust any-one in this damned country. And mind your backs."'

'Yes, a lot of people seem to have said that to us of late. All right, let's get on with it...'

One hour later they were on their way with the two Africans hunched over their wheels, peering through the whirling snow, while next to them, one in each cab, Dickie Bird and Smith worked the newfangled wind-screen wipers by hand, trying vainly to keep the plate of glass clear.

In the back, the men hunched around the big crates which took up most of the space in the two halftracks, with sacks pulled over their heads trying to keep warm the best they could. Most of them had lapsed into a cocoon of silence. It was too much of an ef-fort to attempt to talk in this freezing snow-storm. But the two old shipmates Ginger Kerrigan and Billy Bennett talked and smoked their beloved Woodbines as their halftrack followed the first one, its tracks churning up a white, flying wake behind the vehicle.

Ginger said, 'I think this one is gonna be real hairy, Billy. Won't have much time for the old grumble and grunt.'

'Not much grub either. I can't stomach that raw fish these Swede-bashers scoff.' He sighed and added, 'They're allus hairy ones, Ginger, but the skipper'll get us through like he allus done afore. Him and Mr Bird are real gents.'

Ginger rubbed the snow off his face yet once again. 'Yer,' he agreed, 'I 'spect yer right. But our luck can't hold out for ever–' He stopped short and sat up suddenly. 'Hey, what's that?' he said sharply.

'What's what?'

'I thought I saw someat out there, you great pudden,' Ginger answered and pointed to the left, to where they knew the mountains of central Sweden started to rise.

'And what's the matter with ye, mon?' CPO Ferguson asked, alerted by the sharpness of Ginger's voice.

'I thought I saw something out there, Chiefie.'

'Ye ken what thought did. He thought he'd shat hissen and he had.' The old petty officer laughed at his own humour. 'Weel then, mon, what did ye think ye saw?'

'Something moving fast like we are. Just

144

caught a glimpse of it, Chiefie. Now I've lost it. But I swear I did get a butchers of it.'

CPO Ferguson could see that the young Liverpudlian was not trying to take a rise out of him, as he often did. Ginger Kerrigan was sincere. So he said, 'Och, who'd be out in this wilderness an' in this weather? All the same, we'll keep our eyes peeled.'

'Like tinned tomatoes,' Sparks said cheekily and then fell silent when Ferguson looked at him – hard.

'We can nae afford to take chances. We'll take turns as lookout. You can start off, Kerrigan. First watch.'

'Allus ruddy me!' Ginger exclaimed, but without rancour. He wrapped the sack more closely around his shoulders and then, sheltering behind the cab the best he could, he commenced his watch. But the snowy waste, what he could see of it, remained obstinately empty.

Just before darkness fell, they came to a hamlet; a collection of wooden huts on the edge of a fiord, with upturned boats everywhere and nets hanging up, ready to be mended when the storm abated. But as Jose, who was driving Smith's halftrack, started to slow down, the latter wondered that there was no one in sight. Surely, he told himself,

145

despite the snowstorm there should be somebody in sight. There were no lights in the windows of the huts either. Nor was there any smoke coming from their chimneys.

Smith turned to Jose, hunched over his wheel, his dark face set and intent on driving, for in the soft fresh snow the halftrack tended to skid. 'Jose, have you any idea of how far it is still to Sundsvall?'

Jose flashed a look at his speedometer and did a quick sum. 'He eighty kilometres away perhaps, boss,' he answered, still not taking his eyes off the way ahead.

'Eighty kilometres … that's fifty miles,' Smith said to himself and made his decision. He couldn't subject the men to a night drive in these terrible conditions. Besides it would be too risky. They would see if they could find shelter and some warm food, even if it was only fish, in the lonely hamlet. 'All right, Jose,' he commanded, 'stop over there – near that bigger hut.'

'Don't like him, this place, boss,' Jose said. 'He smell bad.'

Smith laughed softly at the driver's obvious fear. But he told himself there *was* something strange, perhaps even a little uncanny about this little place in the middle of nowhere.

Jose braked to a stop and with a groan of relief, Smith opened the cab door and dropped stiffly to the snow. Behind, the second big halftrack slithered to a halt as well. 'Everybody out,' Smith commanded, wiping the wet snowflakes from his face. 'CPO Ferguson, you stay behind and keep an eye on the halftrack with the drivers, please.'

'Ay ay, sir,' Ferguson answered grimly. 'Ye've got to keep ye eyes on them darkies. They've got thieving ways with them, ye mind.'

Smith shook his head in mock wonder. Then, followed by the rest, he stamped through the ankle-deep snow to the first hut. He knocked on the door. There was no answer. He knocked again. Still no answer. Finally, as all around him the crew shivered and stamped their feet in the freezing cold, Smith turned the door handle.

It opened to reveal a large room, bare of furniture save a table and chairs and a rough couch in the corner. But the place was agreeably warm due to the tiled oven in the corner with a heap of split logs piled up next to it. Hastily Smith walked over to it and felt the tiles. They were still warm. Someone obviously had been heating the stove quite recently.

Dickie Bird pushed in from outside. 'Just had a dekko at the other places – and they're all empty. Bit like the mystery of the *Marie Celeste*, ain't it? And, oh, I found this.' Suddenly his bantering tone had vanished as he held up what he had been carrying behind his back. It was a small axe, probably used for chopping up the firewood for the stoves. But this particular axe had been used for more than chopping up wood, for its blade was red with congealed blood. 'It could have been used for doing some animal to death, or it could…' He didn't finish the sentence, but all of them knew what he meant.

For a long moment there was a heavy silence. Finally Smith broke it with a decisive, 'Well, we're staying here all the same. We'll bunk down in this one hut. We'll post a double sentry, changed every hour, and be on our way at first light tomorrow. Now come on, lads, let's get some of those tins of M and V opened and get a good hot stew going. That'll put some life back into us. We'll wash it down with tea and whisky.' He tapped his pocket which contained his hip flask.

But even Billy Bennett, the crew's glutton, was not cheered up by the prospect of hot food and drink. His face remained as glum and apprehensive as those of the rest. Somewhere outside in the snowy waste a wolf began to howl. Ginger Kerrigan shivered violently and it wasn't just with the cold.

Chapter Six

The two black drivers snored in their cabs beneath piled up blankets and tarpaulins. It was their task to start up the halftracks' engines every two hours so that they wouldn't seize up in the bitter cold. Behind the first halftrack, sheltering the best they could against the bitter wind coming straight from the Artic Circle, Ginger Kerrigan and Billy Bennett, heads buried in the collars of their thick coats, stamped their frozen feet, slapped their arms across their chests and tried to keep their circulation going. It was just after midnight and they had another thirty minutes to go before they were relieved by the two officers, who insisted on sharing the sentry duty with the crew.

Save for the howl of the wind and the snores of the two drivers, all was silent. Even the water of the fiord was hushed, with a sickle moon throwing its spectral light on the abandoned village. 'Gives me the creeps,' Billy Bennett said in a low voice, as if he thought someone might be listening.

'Well, don't exactly make me want to jump with joy,' Ginger replied, staring into the glowing darkness. Up in the mountains a wolf howled again and he added, 'They've even got frigging wolves as well. I tell you, Billy, there's something very fishy about this dump. That axe and then all the people vanished. Where could they go in this kind of weather? And what was it that I saw yesterday?' He wiped the dewdrop expertly off the end of his thin sharp nose and slung it into the snow. 'Very frigging fishy indeed, old matey.'

The minutes passed leadenly. Time and time again the two sentries flashed a look at the green-glowing dials of their wrist-watches in the hope that their spell of duty was up. But that last half hour of their watch seemed to go on for ever.

Ginger Kerrigan looked up for the ump-teenth time when he heard it. The crisp sound of a clawed foot on the frozen surface of the snow. 'Billy,' he whispered, 'there's something out there.'

'Where?' Billy asked in an equally hushed voice.

'To port. Over near the last hut. Can you see it?'

'Yer. Cor ferk a duck! It's a wolf!' Billy exclaimed, as a dark shape slid round the side of the hut and into the patch of hard silver light cast by the moon beyond.

Ginger gasped, then, straining his eyes, he said, 'When did you ever see a wolf with a pack on its back?'

'*What?*'

'Take a gander, Billy. Can you see it now?'

'You're right, Ginger,' Billy replied. 'A box, with like an aerial or something sticking out of it. What d'yer make of it?'

The Alsatian, for that was what it was, heard the voice. It turned its long sloping head in their direction, ears pricked up. It bared its long fangs. A low menacing growl came from deep down in its throat. But for the moment it remained motionless in the snow, staring at them.

Ginger acted. 'Billy,' he said urgently, unslinging his rifle and clicking off the safety catch. 'Go and wake Mr Smith. There's something funny going on here. I don't like the look of it one bit.'

'You're right, Ginger. Watch yersen, old mate.'

'I will. If that ugly brute moves in this

151

direction, he's gonna get a bullet through his skull tootsweet!' Ginger snapped, as Billy, moving with surprising speed for such a heavy man, ran into the hut.

The Alsatian moved. There was something very frightening – even uncanny – about the way it started to approach, dragging its belly low over the snow, yellow eyes fixed with grim intent on the vehicles, and the lone sentry.

Ginger, feeling the small hairs at the back of his head arise with fright, raised his rifle and aimed. The sight must have alarmed the dog, for it stopped and crouched on the snow once more, ears now clapped tightly to its long skull. At that distance Ginger could hear its breath coming in sharp, short gasps. The brute was going to do something dramatic in a moment, he knew that. He'd seen dogs about to spring before. His finger curled, white-knuckled, around the trigger. 'You're for it soon,' he hissed to himself. 'You just try it.'

Behind him the door swung open. Smith came out, blanket wrapped around his shoulders. He took in the scene immediately. 'The Huns used dogs like that on the Western Front in the last show!' he yelled in alarm. 'That's explosive the brute's got on his back … and that aerial thing is intended to set it off, once he's crawled under a vehicle. *Look out. Here he comes!'*

Ginger pressed his trigger. A sharp crack. Two dozen yards away, the snow erupted in a white spurt. He'd missed. Like greased lightning he pulled back the bolt of the Lee Enfield. The empty shell case fell to the ground as he slammed the bolt back again and took aim once more.

Now the Alsatian was only yards away. 'For God's sake don't miss him, now, Ginger!' Smith yelled frantically.

Ginger took first pressure, trying to control his breathing. If he missed now he wouldn't get a second chance. He fired. The dog gave a great howl, leaping up in the air with the pain of the wound. Next instant the explosive packed in the box on its back went up. The Alsatian disintegrated. Blood, fur and bits of flesh flew everywhere. Billy Bennett ducked hastily as the dog's head came sailing by him. 'Christ Almighty, what a turn up for the books!' he gasped as they stared at the dog remains, steaming on the snow.

The explosion had aroused Jose. Now he came stumbling out of his cab, mumbling in Portuguese, to stop transfixed as he saw the mangled carcass of the dead Alsatian.

Hastily he crossed himself and cried, aghast, *'Madre de Dios!'* before cowering back against the side of the cab.

With a shock that went right through to the bone, Smith could see why. Another of the killer dogs was crawling towards the first halftrack, the silver aerial whipping back and forth in the cold moonlight. Smith aimed, fired and missed. All the bullet did was to make the dog cower momentarily on its haunches.

Suddenly Jose moved. What motivated him, they were never able to find out. Was it some wild native instinct that dated back to his youth? Was it only to protect the half-track that had been given into his charge by the Consul at Malmö?

Now he charged towards the crouching dog, yelling at it angrily as if he might frighten it off with the noise, as perhaps he had done as a barefoot boy in his native village. The dog looked bewildered for a moment. Suddenly it bared its yellow teeth, saliva dripping from its fangs. 'Look out Jose!' Smith warned the man urgently. 'Move back – at once!'

But Jose was too enraged. He made shooing motions at the crouching dog. The dog leapt. The metal aerial struck the little black

154

man across the chest as he went reeling backwards, dog on top of him in the snow. For what seemed a long time nothing happened. Then suddenly, startlingly, the box of explosive went up in a great angry red gout of flame and smoke. Jose gave one last agonizing scream, then he was gone, and the dog too. The explosion left the smoking, blackened snow littered with the bloody gore of man and dog like the work of a surgeon abruptly gone mad.

For what seemed an age, the long echoing silence went on, while Smith searched the area for further of the killer dogs. There were none and finally he said, 'The ground's too hard to bury the poor devil. But we must cover the remains – him,' he corrected himself, 'with snow at least.'

'I do,' Pedro volunteered, his black face now almost green.

'I'll gie yon darkie a hand,' CPO Ferguson butted in, gruffly. 'He were nae coward, I ken.'

They didn't sleep any more that night. Instead they huddled in the hut with the wind howling outside, smoking fitfully and occasionally exchanging a few words. All of them were wrapped up in a cocoon of their own thoughts and they weren't pleasant.

They knew that there was someone out there who intended them harm – where would the killer dogs have come from otherwise? But who was it and where was he? They were questions they could not answer, but they were preoccupied with them.

Dawn came at last. It came reluctantly, as if some God on high was hesitant to throw light on the cruel, savage, remote world below. But they were glad of the thin white light. They threw aside their doubts and as a sign of the crew's return to normality, Billy Bennett, the *Swordfish's* glutton, declared as the tea boiled on the stove next to the sausages, sizzling and frying, 'This morning I think I could go the odd banger or two.'

'Or three … or four,' Ginger sneered. 'God strewth, are you gonna make a pig o' yoursen, agen, Billy?'

To which his shipmate gave no reply, for already the fat sailor was chomping on a large pork sausage, the grease running down his chin.

Half an hour later they were on their way again, with CPO Ferguson, after some instruction by Pedro, or 'yon darkie' as the old Scot insisted on calling him, at the controls of the first halftrack, heading through the endless white waste for the port where the

156

coaster would be waiting for them. Now there would be no stops until they reached Sundsvall, for as Smith told Dickie Bird, 'I want to be shut of this bloody awful country, Dickie. And I won't feel safe until we're out of it.'

'My sentiments exactly, old bean. So don't spare the horses, James, what?'

'What indeed!' was Smith's retort.

On the other side of the Baltic at the headquarters of the illegal German naval intelligence service in the northern German port of Flensburg, *Fregattenkapitan* von Horn stared angrily at Goering's signal, while the radio officer who had just brought it in waited in trepidation.

So Goering had failed. By now those damned Englishmen would probably have reached the coast, where, as he already knew from Goering, there was transport waiting to take them to Finland, a country where he had no agents in place and no influence in high places as he had in Sweden. What was he going to do?

He stared out of the window. It was beginning to snow again, soft, sad flakes coming down slowly. Snow usually cheered him up. It reminded him of naked romps in the snow with his fellow cadets as a youngster before the war, wrestling and fooling around, lithe young bodies clasped tightly together. This day, however, the sight of it depressed him, made him feel his own impotence.

The signals officer cleared his throat to remind von Horn that he was still there, awaiting further orders.

Von Horn looked up at him annoyed. 'I know you're there,' he snapped. 'Give me time to think, *mensch*.'

'Sorry, sir.'

Von Horn pondered. It was obvious that the English were heading for Russia. What was there in Finland to interest them? That newly independent little country was too busy trying to get on its feet. The civil war had been disastrous enough for it. It wanted to keep out of all foreign intanglements. So Russia it had to be, and he knew that the Soviet masters of that country would just love to hang, draw and quarter the English for what they had done to the Red Fleet at Kronstadt six years before.

Slowly he began to smile and the waiting lieutenant told himself he had never seen a man whose smile was so evil. An idea was starting to unfurl in his mind. If he, von

Horn, could do nothing in Finland, the Soviets could. There were still plenty of underground Communists in that country.

He nodded to the signals officer. 'I'd like you to take this down.'

Hastily the young officer took out his pad.

'To the Consul General, Petrograd...' He dictated the message slowly, the evil grin still on his narrow face, and then added, 'To be sent in clear.'

'*Klartext, Herr Fregattenkapitan?*' the signals office exclaimed in surprise. 'But the Russians'll pick it up immediately.'

Von Horn looked at him as if he were a halfwit and said triumphantly, 'That's exactly what I want them to do...'

Chapter Seven

It was almost midday before the pale yellow ball of the midday sun rolled over the green swaying horizon to lie there as if too exhausted to rise any further. Occasional little flurries of snow came and went as the little Finnish freighter which would transport them to Finland nosed its way through the ice floes into the port.

On the quayside, now stained yellow with the droppings and urine of horses, taking away the newly caught fish, burly women in heavy clothing filleted the catch, singing all the while in a monotonous chant. There were the usual hangers-on, old men with sticks, a couple of skinny men in leather coats who could have been pimps, watching the freighter come in. But to Smith's practised eye none of them seemed to present any danger.

'What a country,' Dickie cut into his thoughts, 'all ruddy fish. And look at those women. Not a pretty face among 'em. With women like that, I'm surprised the Swedish race didn't die out years ago.'

Smith nodded in a noncommittal manner and searched the deck for the first sight of the wife of this mysterious Mr Reilly. Behind him, Ferguson, who surprisingly enough had struck up a kind of friendship with the 'darkie', was telling Pedro, 'Ay, in Scotland we dinna eat all this fish rubbish. We eat the haggis.'

'Yes, I know of the Scottish men. They wear skirts like the ladies,' Pedro beamed winningly at the dour old Chief Petty Officer.

160

Ferguson ignored the comment. 'Ay, plenty o' good mutton and oats stuffed in a sheep's gut,' he went on, while Pedro shuddered and rolled his eyes dramatically.

'In sheep gut!... That not civilised, boss.'

Relentlessly Ferguson ploughed on with his details of Scottish cuisine.

'That must be her,' Smith said suddenly. 'There you are, Dickie. Just coming down from the bridge.'

'Oh, I say,' Dickie exclaimed. 'What a real cracker! Look at the legs in those riding boots – and by Gad, she's wearing britches. What a delightful little rump!'

'Oh do shut up, Dickie,' Smith said. 'You're always thinking of that.'

'What else is there for a poor sailor chap? Our pleasures are few and far between.'

Smith thought Mrs Reilly striking rather than beautiful. She had a broad, almost Slavic face which glowed with the cold, dark eyes that were the colour of polished chestnuts, firm, painted lips, all underneath a fur hat tilted at a rakish, definitely unladylike angle. Mrs Reilly, Smith told himself, looked like a tough nut.

Twenty minutes later, after the two officers had been introduced and had gone into her cabin, she said, 'Now then Mr Smith, I

161

think we ought to get down to business straightaway.'

Outside, the winches were already beginning to haul up two crates on the freighter's deck while Ferguson, with a wintry smile on his craggy face, was paying Pedro the five sovereigns that Smith had promised the driver, saying, 'Ye're nae bad for a heathen darkie after all.'

'Why, yes,' Smith stuttered, a little startled by Mrs Reilly's directness.

'My husband has the Grand Duke in his charge,' she went on. 'He is making his way from Moscow to Petrograd and I don't need to tell you two where that is. You've been there before.' She puffed out a long stream of smoke from the thin black cheroot she affected.

'Yes,' Smith answered. 'So you know about that business at Kronstadt?'

She nodded, appraising him with those intelligent dark eyes of hers. Suddenly Smith felt slightly embarrassed. For there was something sexually challenging in the look. Did she expect him to make a pass at her or something? he wondered. She crossed her booted legs slowly, provocatively, and continued. 'My husband's problems start really when he reaches Petrograd and attempts to find some way across the Finnish border and then on to the nearest railway station.'

'It's a very long border,' Dickie Bird said, remembering the geography he had learnt at Dartmouth.

'Yes, but at this time of the year he can't go too far north to cross it. It has to be somewhere around the Gulf of Finland, and that,' she said, with a determined look on her striking face, 'is where the Soviets are at their strongest.'

'I see,' Smith said, as the ship's engines started up once more for the crossing to Finland and the anchor chain rattled back into the locker. 'And where do we come in?'

She looked at him again in that same mannered and interested fashion. Once more he felt himself blush. 'The plan remains as it was – for the time being. When we hear from my husband he might suggest we make some changes. My husband is a very impulsive, changeable man.' She stroked her cheek with the back of her hand, as if she were recalling something which justified that statement. 'He never likes to stick to the same routine. He believes it to be dangerous. No matter – we shall see. One thing, however, we must be on our guard all the time. The coastal areas of Finland are safe. But north, where there are the wandering Lapps, there is danger. After the battle of Tammerfors in '18 when the Finnish marshal, von Mannerheim, beat the Red Finns and their Bolshevik backers, the survivors fled into the forests. Now they live from banditry. They live by raiding smaller places, stealing the peasants' food and animals and usually raping their women.'

Dickie Bird flashed Smith a swift look. In polite society back home women didn't talk of rape, but Mrs Reilly hadn't even batted an eyelid at the word.

'They are easily bribed of course, these Red Finns, and as their lives are forfeit if the Finnish Government catches them, they are prepared to take the most amazing risks. So we must watch out for the Red Finns at all times. Now then,' she said finally, giving Smith that strange provocative look once more, 'I shall go back to my cabin. It has been a long trip here and tomorrow we arrive at dawn. There we must start immediately. Time is running out.' She rose and they stumbled to their feet. But she did not make the usual noises that an English-woman of her class would make about sitting down. Instead she nodded as if in approval and went out, her buttocks sway-

164

ing splendidly in those too tight breeches of hers.

Smith waited till she was out of earshot before asking, 'Well, Dickie, what do you make of her?'

Dickie Bird pursed his lips. 'Well, she's a tough bird, that's for sure. No flies on her. But on the whole, Smithie, old bean, I can't weigh her up.' He looked directly at his old shipmate. 'I'll tell you one thing though – for free.'

'What's that?'

Dickie winked knowingly. 'She deucedly fancies *you...*'

Smith was reading an old battered copy of John Buchan's *Thirty-Nine Steps* – 'a ripping good yarn, old chap,' Dickie had said when he had given it to him – lying in his bunk when the knock came at the door of his cabin. By now the freighter was almost half-way there, ploughing through the pitch-black night towards Finland, and he was slowly becoming sleepy, despite the appeal of the 'ripping good yarn'. He frowned. Who could be knocking at his cabin door at this hour? 'Yes?' he said after a moment, realising that he was lying in his bunk, clad only in his shirt, and wondering whether he should get up and pull on a pair of slacks.

The door opened gently and he dropped the book, as if it were red-hot. It was Mrs Reilly, dressed in an ankle-length fur coat, her hair hanging loose down her back, another long black cheroot in her hand. 'May I come in, Mr Smith?' she asked softly and even before he could answer, she was closing the door behind her.

'Why, yes,' he stuttered, wondering what in heaven's name had she to talk to him about at this time of night. 'I'm afraid I can't get up. I'm not dressed.'

She laughed softly. 'I see,' she said. 'But no matter. I shall fetch myself a chair.' She crossed to the corner of the little cabin and, lifting the battered chair which sat there, pulled it to the centre of the cabin. 'May I sit down?' she asked.

'Why, of course,' Smith answered.

As she did so, her fur coat slid open to reveal those excellent legs of hers, clad in sheer black silk stockings. Mrs Reilly made no attempt to cover her legs. Instead she drew at her cheroot, staring at him with an amused look in those dark glistening eyes of hers.

He felt a sudden anger. What was so funny about him? All the same he could not help

166

but notice the odour of her femininity, a mixture of expensive perfume and woman.

For a moment or two they sat thus, the handsome young officer and the striking woman, perhaps only a yard away from each other, the only sound the steady throb of the engines as the old freighter beat its way eastward at five knots per hour.

'Englishmen are so shy,' she said after a while. 'European men, especially Russian, are not so discreet with a woman.'

'I see,' he said, telling himself he sounded an awful fool, but knowing he had to say something.

She crossed her legs once more – carelessly. His heart skipped a beat as he caught a glimpse of the dark patch of hair. She was naked above the stockings!

She saw the look in his eyes and said quietly in a matter-of-fact tone, 'Yes, I'm naked. For you. If you'll have me.' She rose, grasped the fur coat at the collar and dropped it to reveal her full nakedness.

Smith swallowed hard. She was lovely … perfect breasts, tight rounded buttocks, trim waist. She was a mature woman, older than he was, he knew that. But her body was that of an athletic twenty-year-old. 'Can I kiss you?' she asked. Before he could answer she bent over and pressed her mouth against his. He felt the nipples of her breasts brush against his open shirt. Suddenly he was erect and wanted her – wanted her badly.

With her lips glued to his, she slid her hand underneath the blanket and started as she felt his hardness. Now he couldn't stop himself. He put his arms around her naked body and clasped it fiercely to him, his nostrils assailed by the odour of a woman on heat.

Violently he pulled her down upon him. With his foot he pushed away the blanket. She looked and gave a little moan of delight. She spread her legs and slid down on his hardness. Now it was his turn to moan with delight. 'Say you like it,' she hissed feverishly into his ear, as she pumped herself up and down upon him, slowly. 'It gets you? You enjoy it? How does it feel…?' The questions came in harsh gasped phrases, as her tousled hair fell over a suddenly flushed sweating face. 'Make me cry out … come on, hurt me…' Abruptly her spine arched. Her head went back, mouth open and gasping, eyes wild and demented. Next instant she collapsed upon him, and he could feel her heart beating frantically, as if it might burst out of that beautiful ribcage at any moment…

How long she stayed, he didn't remember afterwards. It was a time of hardness and softness, fiery passion and cool sexual calculation, wildness and tenderness. Smith had never known a woman so abandoned, so unconscious of everything but the desire to be taken and satisfied.

Once he thought, in an exhausted pause between their lovemaking, he thought he heard her sob gently. But then minutes later she was caressing his penis once more, planting tiny fevered kisses on his lips, already panting with desire.

Some time that night when they lay in each other's arms, smoking and staring up at the ceiling, she started to speak in a low, unemotional voice, almost as if she were speaking to herself. 'You must take care of yourself, darling. Sidney – my husband – is a strange man. No one really knows what goes on his mind–'

He opened his mouth to ask her what she meant, but she pressed her hand gently over his lips so that he would be silent.

'Do not trust him. He has plans with the boy ... the Romanov boy ... which might be different to yours. I am not an angel ... I know I have betrayed him.' There was a sudden sob in her voice. 'But he has

169

betrayed me many times, not only with women. Take heed, de Vere, take heed.'

He freed his lips to ask what she meant, but already she was running her wet mouth down the length of his lean white body, slowly, seductively, kissing his flesh, licking at it with her tongue, making him tingle with excitement, all thoughts of Sidney Reilly vanished, as he waited for the pleasures to come.

When he awoke, it was nearly dawn and she was gone without trace, as if she had never been there in the first place.

Chapter Eight

On the other side of the River Neva, Trotsky was to speak for the first time since the assassination attempt on his life. Now the workers streamed in their hundreds across the bridge, heading for the hall where the great orator would deliver his speech. Inside the hall, there were hundreds of others, awaiting Trotsky's appearance in noisy expectation.

There was no heat in the great hall. The

stifling heat of unwashed stale bodies muffled in heavy clothing, packed together in tight rows, sufficed however to keep the place warm. Heavy blue smoke from the black tobacco that most of them smoked hung in a heavy cloud beneath the roof. Others were drinking from little flat bottles of vodka. Every now and again an official with a red armband would appear on the stage and plead with the 'comrades' not to smoke or drink. But no one took any notice. They continued the two little pleasures which were the only things that made their miserable lives worthwhile.

In the end the bearded chairman rang his bell for order and slowly the great assembly came to order as Trotsky bustled onto the stage in a great hurry as he always appeared to be. Reilly nudged the boy. 'That's him,' he whispered.

The boy nodded, but he didn't need to be told that this was Trotsky. He had seen him often enough in the flickering newsreels they had shown on Sunday in the village's 'House of Culture', the building from which the party bosses had tried to indoctrinate the reluctant peasants.

Trotsky paused. He surveyed their sweating, under-nourished faces with that quizzing, half-contemptuous look of his, which spoke of limitless, conscious superiority. Trotsky pushed his pince-nez more firmly up his nose with his unwounded arm, tilted his head upwards, twisting around at the same time to push forward his right shoulder – his favourite pose when giving a speech – and began, 'Comrades, we are in a state of great danger. Our beloved leader Comrade Lenin is dying, we all know that. What will happen when he goes? What will be his political testament? Will the Whites and reactionaries again attempt to seize power? What will the West do?...' He rained the questions down upon his increasingly excited audience like hammer blows. 'What is the position of the bourgeoisie?'

'*Doloie boorjoie!*' the working men audience thundered back in an angry base. 'Down with the bourgeoisie!'

'After Lenin's death, we Soviets do not want another war. What would the Soviet state gain from it?' Trotsky went on, the sweat standing out on his high forehead like opaque pearls. 'It is the bloodsucking plutocratic capitalists and their lackeys, whose powdered effete diplomats, who want war. They are the ones who profit from it with their armament factories and chateaux.

They get rich. The working man gets killed.'

His audience loved it. They rose to their feet, clapping their hands above their heads and crying, 'Death to the bloodsuckers and their jackals!'

Reilly stood and clapped with the rest. But already he had forgotten Trotsky and his rabble-rousing speech. His mind was racing electrically on other matters.

He sat down with the rest, wondering if he could really bring it off, one obscure man, born a Jewish bastard in Odessa, against the power of a nation over one hundred million strong. What if the English failed to back him once the deed had been done? He fingered the lock of Napoleon's hair, which was his talisman, in the pocket of his overcoat. Suddenly he grunted, angry at his own doubts. Nothing would go wrong... Trotsky would be assassinated, Stalin would be given the blame and then the time would be ripe for the Russian people to search for a new non-Communist leader. He gazed at the boy from the corner of his eye. He was strong and handsome with those firm blue eyes of his. The people would idolize him.

He ran the plan over his mind once more. He told himself that Napoleon had been an obscure lieutenant of artillery when he had started his bid for power. Why, he hadn't even been a Frenchman, but an Italian born in Corsica. He had virtually conquered the whole of Europe, with his motto of *'L'audace, encore l'audace, toujours l'audace'*. Of course his own boldness would succeed. It always had done throughout the history of the world.

'But in the near future,' Trotsky was saying, his fist clenched dramatically, 'if there is to be a conflict and if you have to suffer, even die, you will do so for your own kind. It will be a workers' war, not for the pluto-capitalists. Comrades, you will be fighting for your state – the soldiers' and peasants' Soviet. *For yourselves!*' he bellowed, his voice hoarse with strain.

Again the audience rose as one and bellowed back the cry Trotsky loved. *'All power to the people!'* The rallying cry echoed and re-echoed around the great hall.

Standing in the shadows at the far end, Cheka cap pulled well down over his face, Aronson smiled cynically to himself. If it came to a fight for the succession, which was Trotsky's real message, he, Trotsky, wouldn't be doing the fighting and dying, he damn well knew that. Trotsky would probably die warm and safe in bed of old age, like all these so-called great leaders had done throughout the ages.

But it must not come to another armed conflict, Aronson told himself. The question of Lenin's successor must be solved by peaceful means. Russia couldn't stand another civil war, with millions of its citizens dying in the process.

His handsome face hardened. Trotsky had to be protected from Stalin, that was his first priority. But the Commissar had also to be protected against the reactionaries like the Black Hundred. He gazed around the mob in the great hall. There were potential killers everywhere, he told himself. They could even be here at this very moment. And then there was the business of Reilly, the arch spy, and this supposed Romanov child.

He had realised immediately that the message to the German consul in clear text was a German plant. But at the same time it was also genuine. The Fritzes wanted him to take up the hunt after they had probably failed to get those two damned elusive Englishmen. So they were on their way to Finland where they would await Reilly and the Romanov, who presumably they would then transport back to that damned remote island of theirs.

His frown deepened. Reilly was pretty old now, he told himself. For thirty years he had worked underground in Russia for the English, spying and shaping policy. Would he miss this last chance of trying to change Russia's destiny?

But Aronson had no answer for that particular question.

'And what do these reactionaries want?' Trotsky was shouting, face glazed with sweat as if it had been smeared with oil. 'I shall tell you, comrades' – Trotsky leaned forward aggressively and stabbed the smoke-filled air with his forefinger – 'they want to bring back the Tsar! They want to bring back the *Okhrana* secret police! They want to bring back the Cossacks and their damned whips! They want to bring back those thrice-damned chains in which we were bound and shipped off to that Siberian hell. Reaction and terror – that is what the reactionaries and their dastardly renegade backers in Western Europe want!' He gasped for breath as if he had just run a great race.

'*Never!*' the crowd shrieked hysterically, knocking over their chairs as they stumbled to their feet, unwashed faces twisted with hate. '*Never!*'

Reilly smiled to himself. Trotsky would

soon learn what the reactionaries could do. Where that silly aristocratic girl had failed, under his direction her comrades of the Black Hundred wouldn't.

'Serge,' he said, as the crowd began to sit down again, 'it is time to go.'

He took the boy's hand and together they pushed their way through the stinking, sweating mob to the door. A blast of icy air hit them, but Reilly didn't notice. His mind was too intent on carrying out the first step of his great plan. For a moment or two he stood there staring at the yellow darkness. The street outside the hall was virtually deserted. There were a couple of what appeared to be drunks from the vodka stall at the end of the road and there was Trotsky's big car parked opposite, with the driver huddled behind the wheel trying to keep warm, the windows misted up with his own breath.

With apparent casualness, Reilly, holding the boy by the hand, walked towards the big black car. It was a prewar Rolls Royce, he noted. The workers' leaders, he told himself cynically, liked to indulge themselves. As he passed the two apparent drunks in the doorway, he nodded. Immediately they detached themselves from the shadows and

177

began to follow him at five metres' distance, as they had agreed upon.

Reilly and the boy stopped. Again he checked the street furtively. There were still just the four of them and the car. Reilly nodded his approval. He took out the half-litre flat bottle of vodka and as he came level with the driver, he stopped again and took a hefty swig, making appreciative noises as he swilled the fiery liquid down. Now the two men were just behind the car.

Inside, the driver licked his lips and suddenly wound the side window down. He looked up at Reilly's dark, hook-nosed face under the fur hat and told himself here was another kike just like his boss. Still the man had some vodka and he was freezing. 'Comrade,' he growled, 'can I buy a hundred grams of vodka from you? I'm frozen to the bone.'

Reilly gave the burly driver and bodyguard a fake smile. 'I should be honoured if Comrade Trotsky's driver would take what's left for nothing.' He tapped his pocket. 'I have another one here. Please.'

Typical Jew, the driver told himself: always fawning, bowing and scraping. All the same he took the bottle, said a quick thank you and wound up the window hurriedly to keep out the freezingly cold air. Thus he didn't hear the slight click to the rear of the Rolls Royce.

Reilly and the boy walked on, more hastily now, while the two others had vanished down an alley. Behind, the driver gurgled at the bottle happily, telling himself that they should have killed off all the Jews before the war, then Russia wouldn't be in the mess it was now.

Reilly stopped under a streetlight and took out his pocket watch. He looked at its dial under the yellow flickering light of the gas jet.

'Why do you want to know the time now, Mr Reilly?' Serge asked.

Reilly looked down at him. 'Because soon – in ten minutes, to be exact – something will happen which will change Russia, perhaps make you a great leader. We will see. Come on, Serge, my boy.' He gripped the boy's hand more firmly. 'We have things to do yet.'

'So, comrades, I conclude,' Trotsky said, feeling his shirt sticking to him unpleasantly with sweat, 'with this. There are hard times ahead of us. But we shall overcome them. But how shall we overcome them?' He paused rhetorically.

In the dark aisle, Aronson glanced at his watch. Trotsky was due to finish in five minutes precisely. Then he, Aronson, had to see him back safely to his headquarters of the Smolny Institute on the other side of Petrograd.

'I shall tell you,' Trotsky answered his own question. 'By solidarity. By being ever-vigilant. By being constantly ready to take up the challenge from wherever it may come to our Soviet state–'

'*Kleba!*' a drunken voice broke into the flow of rhetoric. 'The workers must have bread, Comrade Trotsky!'

Trotsky was taken by surprise. 'Did you say – bread?' he stuttered.

'*Da, Tvaorivitch. Kleba,*' the drunk, who looked as if he might be some sort of dockworker, yelled doggedly.

'How can we fight the reactionaries and all the rest if we don't get enough to eat?' the drunk persisted as the Cheka men started to work their way through the mob to get to him and take him away.

Aronson looked at his watch. Trotsky was overrunning. He wished him to get down from the stage. But he knew the Commissar; he could never refuse a challenge like this from the audience. He'd have to bring the rabble, who looked as if they were now beginning to agree with the drunk, round to his way of thinking. He had to leave the meeting with the mob cheering him. 'Well, let me say this to you, comrade. Under the new Five Year Plan–' Trotsky never finished his attempt to explain how much wheat was being harvested under the Plan.

From outside there came the boom of a tremendous explosion. The door blew open. A hot wave of blast burst through it. And then Aronson was running, automatic already in his hand.

On the stage Trotsky was yelling urgently, *Reactionaries … assassins!*' But nobody was listening to Trotsky now. They were all too busy trying to save their own skins; and even as he ran through the door into the smoke-filled street outside, followed by the panicked mob, Aronson told himself the people he was trying to save were a spineless bunch. Then he stopped dead, with him the first of the mob.

Chapter Nine

Even Aronson was shocked, as behind him the crowd of escapees gave a great collective 'Aw…' He had seen many terrible things in the Revolution and the Civil War which had followed, but the scene which presented itself in the street that ran along Neva was horrific. Trotsky's car lay shattered, all four tyres burst, thick white smoke pouring from its ruptured engine. The force of the impact had burst the car's roof above the driving seat and propelled the driver through it. Now he hung legless and headless and totally naked from one of the skeletal trees like some kind of obscene human fruit!

Aronson took in the situation at once. If Trotsky had not been delayed by the drunk and his demand for bread, he would be hanging up there dead, too, now. He didn't hesitate. He knew swift action was needed. He pulled out his Cheka whistle and blew three shrill blasts on it: it was a signal only to be used by senior officers of the secret police. Immediately those Chekists who had been trying to control the crowd stopped and came running in his direction. 'Seal off the whole area,' he commanded while they were still running. 'No one is to leave the scene. One of you, get my car and alert HQ. The frontier to Finland is to be closed forthwith. No one is to leave the country in that direction.' He rapped out order after order until Trotsky interrupted him in a dazed voice, asking, 'What has happened, comrade?'

Aronson thought the question was un-necessary; still, he told the bemused Commissar, adding, 'Your life is in extreme danger, Comrade Trotsky. I must place you under Cheka guard at once.' He nodded to the two policemen closest to him. 'Escort Comrade Trotsky to the nearest police box, request a car to be sent there at once and take him to HQ.' He looked sternly at the two Chekists. 'You will answer to me with your heads if anything goes wrong.' As an afterthought he took out his second pistol and handed it to a surprisingly speechless Trotsky. 'Here you are, Comrade, use it if necessary.'

Trotsky let himself be led away while Aronson walked briskly over to the smoking car. He knew immediately what had happened. Someone had placed a bomb under the vehicle's rear axle – a time bomb, timed to go off as soon as Trotsky had entered. But who had placed it there? He pulled out his torch and flashed around the area. There were bits of black metal from the shattered Rolls Royce everywhere. With his foot he turned them over here and there, searching for clues. He frowned. Not much to go on, he told himself. Then he had it. A piece of steel, not the sheet metal used to make the Rolls Royce. He picked it up and winced. It was still hot.

He flashed his torch closer on it, screwing up his eyes as he tried to make out the three letters stamped onto the bit of metal, which had obviously come from the bomb which had destroyed the car. *B ... S ... A ...* he deciphered the letters. He whistled softly. 'British Small Arms Company,' he said to himself.

The English were behind the attempt on Trotsky's life, not Stalin. That could mean only one thing. *Reilly!*

Forgetting the freezing cold, Aronson tried to pull the various strands together. Reilly was in Petrograd, of that he was sure. Because it would be here that the power struggle would take place once Lenin died.

Aronson was sure, too, that the elusive British spy was behind this latest attempt on Trotsky's life. The question was, now that the would-be murder had failed, would he stay in Petrograd?

He spotted a police car, crowded with heavily armed militia. He flagged it down and without hesitation turfed out one of the militiamen to make room for him and ordered the driver to take him to Cheka HQ at once. Even as they drew up at the Smolny Institute, once a school for the daughters of the aristocracy and upper class, he knew that something was wrong. Everywhere the lights blazed, although the day shift had gone home long ago. Motorcycle messengers were roaring to and fro. Telephones jingled.

Hurriedly he climbed up the steps and called to the duty officer. 'What's the matter?' he demanded. 'Has something gone wrong?'

The duty officer clicked to attention. To his surprise, Aronson could see the man had tears in his eyes. 'Comrade, it has happened, finally,' the man said in a thick voice.'

'*What,* man?' Aronson barked impatiently.

'Comrade Lenin, comrade ... he's dead,' the duty officer stammered, tears now rolling down his hard face.

Aronson took the steps to his office at the double. There, he picked up the phone and called for Ilona down in the radio room. A minute later she appeared, cheeks flushed, bearing a piece of paper. She attempted to give it to him but he caught her wrist, handsome face hard and impatient. 'Did he appoint a successor? Is it that monster, Stalin, or Trotsky?'

She shook her pretty head. 'No, neither … and you're hurting me!'

'Sorry,' he said and released his grip. 'Neither,' he echoed her words. 'That's impossible. *Yo tuoyu mat!*' He spat out the obscene Russian curse angrily. 'What a fine mess Russia will be in now.' His eyes fell on the piece of paper. 'What's that?'

'Our friends in Moscow managed to get some insight into Lenin's political testament. This is part of it. Here.'

Hastily he grabbed the sheet of paper. His eyes flew across Lenin's last words. 'Comrade Stalin, having become a general secretary, has concentrated, tremendous power in his hands, but I am not sure he knows how to use that power properly… Stalin is too rough… Therefore I propose that the comrades find a way to remove Stalin from that position…'

Aronson looked up momentarily and laughed bitterly. 'What a blind fool Lenin was. Did he think, with the power that he has in his hands, that Stalin would tamely allow himself to be shuffled off to his native Georgia or somewhere?'

He bent his head once more and read on. 'On the other hand, Comrade Trotsky is distinguished not only by his exceptional abilities – he is the most able man in the committee – but also by his too far-reaching self-confidence and a disposition to be too much attracted by the purely administrative side of affairs.'

Aronson flushed angrily. He dashed the paper angrily to his desk with so much force that the telephone bell rattled. 'What an idiot!' he exclaimed. 'In essence, Lenin has appointed no one to succeed him.'

'What does that mean?' she asked, a little bewildered.

'It means that the way is open now for an all-out power struggle between Stalin and Trotsky,' he snapped. 'It means that Russia might be plunged into civil war once more. It means that the way will soon be open for Reilly and his backers, the English, to impose their will on Mother Russia and put forward this supposed Romanov survivor as the country's saviour.' He sighed like a man sorely tried. *'Boshe moi,* what a country!'

She bent over and kissed him gently on the cheek. 'You are a good man,' she said huskily and he could see the tears in her eyes now.

'Thank you, Ilona. But what Russia needs today is *hard* men. Men who finally organise our poor benighted people into an organized, purposeful nation.'

Ilona dropped her hand to his lap. Gently Aronson pushed it away. 'Thank you again, Ilona. But not tonight. I must think, use all my powers of concentration. Mother Russia must be saved.' He looked up and as she turned to go, she saw the look of absolute, total despair in his eyes. Sadly she went out...

Five versts away in a hired *droschki* heading steadily northwest through the falling snow, Reilly had despaired too for a while. Again the assassination of Trotsky had failed. But he had immediately cheered up when he heard the news of Lenin's death in his sleep. That information had cancelled out his disappointment.

Next to him, the boy, wrapped in an old fur rug by the coachman, slept, his head against Reilly's shoulder. As he looked down at him he wondered again how the boy had escaped. Back in that terrible year of the Revolution some horrific things had happened to the aristocrats and the upper class. Reilly had been shocked, terribly shocked, at the rape of aristocratic ten-year-olds; at the Tsarist officers whose broad epaulettes had been nailed to their shoulders by their mutinous soldiers, with the men then cutting off their testicles and thrusting them into the dying officers' mouths; at the slaughter of elderly ministers, whose beards had been torn from their faces with the flesh still attached before they were pushed into the sewage holes to drown in ordure.

That had been in the beginning. But his initial horror at the Revolution had given way to the realisation that here was the opportunity he had always sought – the opportunity for greatness in the manner of his hero, Napoleon.

But what a frustrating, heartbreaking task it had been! The Russians were a lazy, disorganised people, allowing themselves to be trodden on by those in power because they didn't seem to have the will to fight back. Instead, they fled into alcohol and depravity.

How much time and money he had spent

getting the counter-revolutionaries organized. Those anti-Semites of the Black Hundred were good at talking, but seemingly incapable of putting a plan into operation. The English under 'C' were slow and too cautious, though people like Churchill and Hozier had gingered them up a little. But in the end he had convinced them that his plan, the little he had told them of it, was workable.

Now at last his years of working and waiting were coming to fruition. The pawns were all in their places – C, the two young naval officers, his wife, and the boy. Reilly sat back in the padded coach, listening to the tinkling bells of the three horses pulling the coach, a little tired but happy. *The great game could commence!*

BOOK THREE

ESCAPE OR DIE

Chapter One

At a dead slow crawl, the Thorneycrofts purring softly, the torpedo boats had approached the shallows at Kronstadt in a V formation. To their right the inky sky had been lit up time and time again by scarlet flashes as the Bolshevik gunners had fired at the Navy biplanes which were carrying out the feint. Smith had told himself the fly-boys were really giving the Russkis some stick.

Then suddenly, startlingly, there was a huge flash of light which had revealed the whole of the Red Fleet, silhouetted against the lights of Petrograd. 'Get a butchers o' that, sir!' Ginger Kerrigan had cried excitedly. 'There they are!' He'd been right. There had been their targets.

'Ahead both ... full speed ahead!' he had cried joyously, carried away by the excitement of the kill to come.

The *Swordfish* had surged forward. A huge white wake erupted behind her. Her prow rose in the air. Each wave they hit felt as if it were a brick wall.

Searchlights clicked on in the enemy fleet. Red flares had sailed into the night sky. From port a machine gun had begun firing. Angry white tracer had come hurrying towards the attackers. It had been followed a moment later by the throaty bark of a quick-firer. Water had started to erupt in wild crazy fountains all about them. But they had stuck to their course, hurtling forward across the surface of the water at 40 knots.

Then Dickie Bird had spotted her, their target. 'The *Spartak!*' he had yelled frantically above the ear-splitting racket made by the Thorneycroft engine. 'To port there!'

Smith had recognized her immediately. There had been no mistaking the three funnels of the old Tsarist battleship. Now he had pressed every last bit of speed out of the *Swordfish,* which was groaning at every seam, as if she might fall apart at any moment. '*Stand by the tubes!*' he had yelled.

Ginger and Billy Bennett had run to their posts, staggering all over the racing deck.

Six hundred yards! It was now or never, he had told himself. To his front there had been scarlet flashes everywhere as the Red Fleet took up the challenge. '*Fire!*' he had yelled.

'*One ... two....!*'

The *Swordfish* had shuddered as the first one-ton torpedo had hit the water. A moment later it was hissing through the harbour towards its target. Number two followed with a splash and a ripple of bubbles and then it, too, was on its way towards the trapped *Spartak*. Smith had swung the boat round in a great racing curve and then they had been belting out of the harbour, with shells exploding all around them, the air singing with great shards of bright silver metal. The *Swordfish's* mast had come tumbling down. Billy Bennett had groaned and had slumped to the deck, blood jetting from his wounded arm. Wildly Smith had swung the boat from left to right in crazy zigzags, trying to put the Russian gunners off.

Then it had happened. A great hollow boom, followed an instant later by a blinding scarlet flash which had coloured the racing sea in its blood-red hue. Smith had flung a hasty glance over his shoulder, his heart beating furiously with excitement.

He cried with sheer joy at what he saw. The *Spartak* had been struck midships. Already, panic-stricken sailors were diving over the side into the boiling sea. A sailor dived from the top mast where he had been the lookout, missed the water, hit the side of the listing battleship and then crumpled into the sea like a sack of wet cement.

Suddenly there was a great, tearing, ear-splitting rending of tortured plates. Slowly but definitely the crippled battleship had begun to turn like some enormous whale in its death throes. Loud gurgling sounds came from it like water running down a drain, followed by obscene belches as trapped pockets of air broke the surface.

An underwater explosion had ripped the keel off the *Spartak*. Blazing oil had poured out of her in a frightening scarlet stream, en-gulfing the frantic, screaming men in the water in a flash. Slowly, majestically, the Soviet battleship completed a full circle, her propellers dripping and gleaming in the blood-red glare. For a few seconds the *Spartak* had poised thus, her insides being torn apart by the inrushing water and repeated explosions as her ammunition locker had gone up, the metal hull glowing a dull angry red. Another explosion. With a great lingering, sad sigh, what had been left of the *Spartak* had slid slowly beneath the surface of the water, leaving the oily water behind her frothing and fuming. The pride of the new Soviet Fleet had been destroyed...

Now as the old freighter came to a stop in the harbour and Smith gazed out at the stretch of water which led to Petrograd, where he had earned his VC for sinking the *Spartak*, he thought how he had changed since 1918. Then, although he had been a veteran of the naval battles in the Straits of Dover, he had been a relative innocent. Now, after six years of working together with C and his Secret Service, he was anything but innocent.

He looked up to where Mrs Reilly, as he still called her even though they were lovers, was dealing with the Finnish skipper, and told himself that now he even took and seduced other men's wives. He sighed and wondered idly if there was any way of turning the clock back. What if he hadn't tackled the *Spartak?* Perhaps if the admiral then in command had given him another target, a lesser ship, he might have remained an obscure lieutenant, destined to serve his thirty years and retire to the Home Counties as a lieutenant commander, instead of becoming 'Common Smith VC' whose name and medal were familiar to every newspaper reader in the country.

'A penny for them?' Dickie Bird asked,

coming up from below, muffled up in a thick civilian greatcoat, with a scarf tied around his neck against the biting cold. He looked at his old shipmate curiously as if he already suspected something had gone on between him and the beautiful Mrs Reilly. But before Smith could answer, the woman called down from the bridge. 'Mr Smith, could you get your crew ashore as soon as possible? The captain here will supervise the unloading of the two crates. We expect the locomotive to be here at any minute.' She made a counting gesture in the continental fashion with her thumb and forefinger.

'Cripes!' Dickie Bird exclaimed. 'The old Horsemen of St George do work, don't they! Now we're going to have a private train...'

'Gentlemens and lady, the locomotive,' the fat little Finnish train driver with the Bronx accent announced in his fractured English, sweeping off his battered leather cap and bowing, as if he expected a round of applause.

The little party stared in awe at the ancient engine, its sides covered with rust, the tender piled with logs, with, beyond, two flat cars laden with the crates and behind them a small passenger coach, its sides still marked by bullet holes from Finland's civil war of six years before.

'Gawd ferk a duck!' Billy Bennett exclaimed, breaking their awed silence. 'What is it – Stephenson's frigging *Rocket?*'

The fat little Finn, who Ginger had already christened 'Finnegan' because he could not pronounce the driver's long and complicated name, rubbed the side of the great old locomotive with his greasy rag and said proudly, 'Best English make. Look!' He pointed to a plate, set in the side of the cab.

Dickie Bird peered at it and read out the legend, 'Manufactured ... York Carriage Works ... 1882... Oh, my sainted aunt, it *is* old! Do you think it'll manage to get us there?'

'Gentleman's sainted aunt need no fear... She'll get gentlemens – and lady – there.' He patted the side of the locomotive, as if it were a pedigree horse.

Smith smiled and said, 'All right, chaps, let's get aboard. Can't hang about here all day.' He shot a look over his shoulder at the still green waters of the Gulf of Finland, remembering the last time he had been here before the attack on the *Spartak*. Suddenly he shuddered, and it wasn't with the cold. A lot of good men, both British and Russian, had died that time. Was history going to repeat itself?

Half an hour later they were on their way, chugging eastwards through the empty wastes of Finland at a steady ten miles an hour, the locomotive trailing thick clouds of black smoke behind it. For the most part, the men mostly dozed, though a few played cards; for like sailors all over the world, they were not interested in the scenery. They had seen enough of it in their past travels.

Smith and Dickie Bird were seated up front with Mrs Reilly in that part of the carriage which had been curtained off to give her some privacy from the men. Now she told them what she knew and gave them their instructions for the journey till they reached the port where *Swordfish* would be reassembled, ready for action. 'The captain of the Finnish ship translated the local Finnish paper for me,' she explained, as they rattled through the empty countryside weighted down with snow, with the firs marching in silent ranks to the horizon as far as the eye could see. 'The headline was that Lenin is dead and that there has been another attempt on Trotsky's life which was naturally the work of my husband.'

'Oh, I say!' Dickie Bird gasped.

'It failed,' she said laconically. 'At all events, things are obviously coming to a head at Petrograd now. We must be ready to play our part. The crisis, I am sure, will come soon. For my husband, it is his last chance to achieve greatness. He is getting old.'

She looked at Smith, who blushed when he thought of what they had done the night before and said, her face revealing nothing, 'You can see how lonely this dreary country is, nothing but snow and trees. We could be attacked anywhere along the route until we get to the port. Your men will have to be on guard, Mr Smith.'

'The Chief Petty Officer has already broken out weapons. They are all armed, Mrs Reilly. And that fellow with the golf bag you saw earlier on, Ginger Kerrigan? Well, it contains our Lewis gun. I think we can manage.'

'Good,' she said in a brisk, businesslike manner. 'Then I shall let you get on with your duties.' They were dismissed.

The morning passed slowly. Outside, the wilderness remained empty, save for wild snow hares who stared at the metal monster crawling by, long ears quivering, and an occasional stag, muzzling at the snow, trying

201

to find vegetation below, his nostrils steaming greyly. But even in this snowy waste there were a few villages, a huddle of white clapboard houses around the station, where the train would be halted so that the stationmaster could come aboard and ask the passengers if their 'Honours' would give permission for the train to proceed. According to Mrs Reilly the custom dated back to the days when Finland had been ruled by the Tsar and only high Tsarist officials travelled in a private first-class coach. Hence their privileged treatment. 'Crikey!' Ginger Kerrigan exclaimed when he heard that. 'We ain't half a lot of Lord Mucks now!'

Ferguson shot him a hard look but he had no effect on the ginger-haired Liverpudlian. Now, when he fetched a mug of steaming tea from the samovar which was kept boiling on its stand at the end of the coach, he'd say in what he thought was an upper class accent to Billy Bennett, 'I say, William, will you pass me the sugar, old thing?' and drink his tea with his little finger sticking out in a refined manner. So he imagined at least.

But not all the Finnish stationmasters in their frock coats and leather cross-strap were so polite. Some fifty kilometres west of Lahti just as the sun was beginning to set, colouring the white steppe with a blood-red hue, the little fat driver, his face as black as any negro's from the flying soot, stopped at a tiny village to load the tender up with fresh logs. As in the other villages the station-master entered the carriage, cap in hand. But this village stationmaster was scruffy and unshaven in contrast to the others. He hung his head to one side as if he didn't want them to see the shifty look in his dark eyes.

Mrs Reilly spoke to him in Russian and translated his answer. 'He says he has orders from further up the line not to let any train through till tomorrow morning. An urgent repair is being carried out, it seems.'

Dickie looked out at the darkening snow-field and said, 'It's going to be pretty parkey inside here tonight without the heat from the engine.'

Smith looked at the little Finnish engin-eer. 'Haven't we got enough wood to keep on going a bit? I don't trust this fellow.' He nodded at the stationmaster with his hang-dog face.

'Me neither,' he answered in that thick Bronx accent of his. 'But not possible, gentlemens. Not enough wood.'

Smith turned to Mrs Reilly again. 'Would

you ask him if he could find us some warm accommodation for the night?'

She did so and translated that the stationmaster was offering them two huts next to the rusty branch line which ran behind the station.

'Then that will have to do,' Smith said reluctantly, taking out a sovereign and giving it to Mrs Reilly. 'Give him this and ask if he can't rustle up some warm food for us.'

The stationmaster's dark eyes lit up when he saw the gold coin. His face was transformed. He gave them a fake smile and then he was backing his way down the aisle, bowing and scraping mightily, while Dickie Bird moaned, 'I 'spect we'll get fleas...'

Chapter Two

'Finnegan,' Ginger Kerrigan asked, Woodbine, dangling out of the side of his mouth. Outside it was already dark and the temperature had dropped dramatically as they huddled around the crackling wood stove. 'What do you think of that stationmaster?'

By way of answer, the little train driver drew a dirty finger across his throat. 'Bad man,' he growled, chewing on the raw cod which the stationmaster had brought them and which the crew of the *Swordfish* had refused on sight. 'I tink he Red. Bad man.'

Ginger pondered the information as Billy Bennett asked, 'Why can't we get loaded up with logs and do a bunk, Finnegan?'

Sitting at the other side of the hut, Dickie Bird said, 'Yes, why can't we?'

The Finn swallowed the rest of the raw fish and licked his dirty fingers as if he had just devoured a great delicacy. ''Cos, gentlemens, he's got the key to–' He fumbled for the word, couldn't find it and made a gesture as if pulling something back with both hands.

'Ye mean the switch, man?' CPO Ferguson prompted, with a look in his grey eyes which said, Why can't yon ruddy foreigner speak English?

'Yes, switch to change–' Again he fumbled for the word, and like a man sorely tried, Ferguson said, 'The points.'

Finnegan beamed and nodded.

'Well then, we'll knock him over the jolly old bean,' Dickie Bird said brightly, 'and make a run for it.'

'Good idea, gentlemens,' Finnegan agreed. 'But the telegraph' – he meant the signal telegraph which linked the stations together – 'one of his mens could telegraph up the line. The bandits – they tap line. Know we coming.' He thrust his filthy forefinger up his nose, pulled something out, looked at it as if it were of some importance and then flicked it way with his forefinger and thumb.

There was silence in the hut, while outside the wind howled and shrieked, making the flame of the petroleum lamp which illuminated the place tremble and flicker, casting their shadows in wavering magnification on the walls. Dickie wished that Smith was there, helping to work this thing out. But he was with the woman in the other hut, talking about the plans for the morrow ... or something.

It was Billy Bennett, not regarded as the brightest of the *Swordfish's* crew, who came up with the idea. 'If Finnegan here,' he jerked a thumb like a hairy sausage at the train driver, 'can produce a hawser or stout piece of wire, we could sling it over the telegraph wire. Once we move off, the telegraph comes down and it's Bob's yer frigging uncle.'

'Why didn't I think of that!' Dickie Bird

exclaimed in delight. 'What a splendid wheeze that would be!'

Ferguson looked pained. In the Royal Navy, he told himself, officers and gentlemen should not talk like that, but then again he had never understood officers.

Dickie turned his attention to the Finn who was now biting the black oily grime from beneath his nails with his front teeth. 'Well, have you got any wire, Finnegan?'

'Sure gentlemans, I have.'

'Right then,' Dickie Bird said. 'As soon as that rascal of a stationmaster thinks we've settled down for the night, we'll act. We'll take our weapons. But I think we ought to refrain from firing unless it's absolutely necessary. So we'll look around for some sort of cosh thing.'

'All ye need, sir,' Ferguson broke in, 'is a sock.'

'A *sock?*' they chorused as one.

'Ay,' the old Scot said in that dour manner of his, 'I mind the many a time when I've made one out of a sock when I've been in a tight corner. Now gie heed, this is the way you do it...'

In the other hut, as the crew of the *Swordfish* prepared to break out of that remote railway station, Smith and Mrs Reilly made love. There was no bed and she had refused to lie on the cold stone floor. So now she was sprawled across the rough wooden table, her dress thrown up about her naked waist while he pumped furiously at her from behind. It was rough and brutal, but the very roughness and brutality seemed to excite her. 'More!' she gasped... 'Stick in more!... Oh please, *deeper and harder!*'

Gasping like an asthmatic, his face crimson with the effort, Smith did as she ordered. His fingers bit cruelly into the soft white flesh of her hips as he pumped himself into her, in and out, in and out, with ever increasing fury. It was almost as if he were angry with her. She, too, choked and moaned, as if being subjected to some terrible torture. It wasn't a lovemaking; it was a coupling – of animals on heat rutting – and Smith knew it. But the desire was so great that he had to and he knew she had to as well.

Suddenly she gave a loud groan. Her body tensed convulsively and went slack in the same instant that he achieved his own fulfil-ment, slumping over her half-naked body, all energy drained out of him as if a tap had been opened and allowed it all to go.

For one long moment they lay thus, then he raised himself and pulled up his trousers.

Slowly she turned. She didn't bother to pull down her dress. Instead she sat there, revealing all her delightful nakedness, staring at him with those glowing dark eyes of hers, as if she were seeing him for the very first time. Outside all was quiet save for the howl of the night wind in the forest and the slither of snow as it was blown down.

Finally she broke the heavy silence. 'De Vere, I know I am not for you. Your life is very different from what mine will be.' Suddenly, surprisingly, she took his right hand and pressed it lovingly to her hot cheek. 'But you have been very good to me. I've needed someone like you for a long time.'

Smith blushed and gently freed his hand. 'You've been tremendously good to me, too. But your husband—'

She held up her hand for silence and pulled down her dress. 'Sidney Reilly and I are finished, de Vere. I shall help to get him and the boy out of Russia and back to England – if that is his intention. Thereafter, our ways will part. I have a small private income from my mother's estate, and I can work if necessary.'

'Where will you go?' he asked, telling himself it was about time he got back to the others.

'Africa, South America…' She shrugged those pretty shoulders of hers carelessly. 'Anywhere away from this accursed Europe of ours. I'm sick of it and its wars and revolutions.' She started to tie up her sheer black silk stockings with the frilly red garters that had definitely come from Paris.

'England was all right,' Smith, the patriot, said stoutly. 'I think we've got a pretty good show going back home.'

'England was all right before the Great War. But I fear she, too, is going into a decline. The war took the heart out of the old country. But no matter.' She was businesslike once more, hiding those delightful legs of hers under the long velvet skirt. 'We must get out of this place before dawn, de Vere.'

'I know. My chaps are working on it right now.' He kissed her. 'Now lock the door after me and wait for me to come back and let you know what the plan is.'

She smiled at him wryly and wordlessly opened her purse. Inside there lay an ivory-handled .22 pistol. 'I can defend myself,' she said. 'I wouldn't hesitate to put a bullet through that rogue's heart.'

Smith went out, telling himself what a strange, passionate woman Mrs Reilly was.

She was as tough as nails, yet at the same time she seemed to him very vulnerable. What a life she must have led with this Sidney Reilly!

Slowly, thoughtfully, he walked across to the other hut, feet crunching over the frozen snow. An icy wind blew across the forest and not a light burned in the little settlement. It was obvious that they went to bed with the chickens in these parts. Just as he was about to open the door of the hut, he thought he heard a sound – a horse whinnying. He cocked his head to the wind and listened hard. Nothing... After a moment, he gave up. He went inside, glad of the cheerful warmth after the freezing cold outside.

The men looked at him a little curiously, he thought. But he brushed away his sudden inhibitions and said briskly, 'Well?'

Swiftly Dickie Bird explained the plan. When he was finished, Smith nodded his approval and said, 'All right, let's get started. All hands to action stations. We'll load the logs first. And p.d.q.'

'Pretty damned quick indeed,' Ginger agreed. 'It'd freeze the goolies off'n yer out there now.'

Ten minutes later they had filled the tender and, huddled beneath an old tarpaulin, the

211

Finnish driver raised steam almost noise-lessly, concealing the flames that came from the open firebox as they shoved logs into its greedy red maws. Meanwhile Ginger had clambered up the end of the second flat car and, muffled to the eyes, set up the ugly Lewis machine gun. Smith dropped from the cab and said to Mrs Reilly, who was to accompany him in case any talking was to be done, 'Are you sure you want to come?'

'I'm sure,' she said firmly and CPO Ferguson, with the sock filled with earth, nodded his approval.

'All right, off we go.'

They started to move over the frozen snow, crouched low and hardly daring to breathe, as behind them Billy Bennett, using the hawser like a cowboy's lasso, tossed the heavy metal rope effortlessly over the telegraph wire.

Now the three of them were outside the stationmaster's tumbledown house. All was silent. Nothing stirred save a shutter swinging back and forth in the wind. Gingerly, Smith tried the door. It opened. They passed through. A pile of clothing lay on the rough sofa. From behind the door of the next room came the squeaking of rusty bedsprings.

CPO Ferguson pulled a face. 'Yon man's fornicating – at this time o' night!'

In spite of the tension, Smith grinned and whispered, 'Search those pants. See if you can find the key.'

Hurriedly the old Scot, who knew about such things, rifled the man's pockets while they stood guard. There was no sound inside the house save that of the rusty bedsprings. Smith whispered in Mrs Reilly's ear, 'I suppose that's the only kind of entertainment they have in this Godforsaken place.'

She giggled softly.

Five minutes later they were on their way back with the key for the points switch.

Now things happened fast. The Finnish driver let out sand and gravel onto the line, just in case it was iced up. He didn't want to slip his wheels once he opened the throttle. Up ahead, brawny Billy Bennett opened the points back to the main line and doubled back heavily to the waiting train.

The Finnish drive opened the throttle. Steam gushed up from the outlet. The wheels clattered on the slippery tracks, caught and started to move the little train. 'Hold on your hat!' the driver cried cheerfully over the clatter and the hiss of escaping steam. They started to move forward.

Over in the stationmaster's house, the lamp was suddenly illuminated. There was a cry of rage. A shot rang out. A dark figure pelted across the track to where the telegraph shed was. Ginger Kerrigan ripped off a burst – and missed. Frantically Billy Bennett looked upwards at the cable with the hawser around it. 'Come on, yer sod!' he cursed as the wires obstinately refused to break. *Crack!* Next instant they came tumbling down in a flurry of angry blue sparks.

The train started to gather speed. The Finn opened the throttle wider. Steam gushed upwards. The wheels clattering round and round, driving the pistons to and fro with ever-increasing energy. Billy Bennett clambered up on the tender. With his brawny arms he slung log after log into the cab. With one hand the Finn concentrated on the controls, kicking the logs closer to the firebox for when he needed them. 'Hot dickety!' he kept chortling over and over again as if it were some kind of litany.

Smith craned his neck. Lights were flashing in the firs. Were they a signal? He didn't know. All he knew was that wild firing was erupting on both sides of the track. Whoever the rascally stationmaster had been in touch with had been preparing to ambush them on the morrow. He shouted to the driver, 'Come on, Finnegan, give her all you've got!'

On the flat car, Ginger Kerrigan opened up with his Lewis gun once more. Scarlet flame stabbed the night. Tracer sailed through the darkness like glowing golfballs.

Answering bullets pattered off the side of the locomotive like heavy tropical raindrops on a tin roof. Then they were through the hamlet, heading for the open spaces once more, trailing huge black clouds of smoke behind them. They had done it again. Minutes later they had vanished into the darkness.

Chapter Three

Staraya Derevnya was a shabby little village, consisting of second-rate villas, timberyards and logmen's huts, overlooking the Gulf of Finland. Now in winter with the Gulf almost frozen over it was the bleakest of places, swept constantly by blizzards, coming in relentlessly from the dreaded ice-desert. Here you couldn't tell where the land ended

215

and the sea commenced, for both were blanketed by a thick layer of snow. In the old days Reilly had liked nothing better than to don a pair of skis and glide gently over that frozen waste of water and then, miles out, lie down and listen to the exquisite silence.

He had thought the place the best of all hiding places until he could put his plan into operation. It was near enough to Petrograd to reach the great city in a hurry once the balloon had gone up. Yet, at the same time, it wasn't the place to be visited at this time of the year by any nosey strangers. As for the few residents, their palms had already been well greased and they were prepared to keep their noses out of his, Reilly's, business.

But two days after he and the boy had reached Staraya Derevnya, the 'old village', Reilly had been forced to change his mind. The second attempted assassination of Trotsky had obviously aroused the authorities to extraordinary efforts. There were foot and cavalry patrols everywhere. Twice the village had been visited by a motor patrol of the Cheka and each house been searched. Fortunately he had been warned in time and he had taken the boy out on skis far into the Gulf of Finland until the patrol had

216

gone. But Reilly had survived so long because he was always alert to the next possible threat. His guess was that the Cheka would soon start a series of night patrols, moving into the outlying villages where they suspected the would-be killers were hiding at four or five in the morning when it was still pitch-black and the suspects would still be fast asleep.

So he had made his preparations. He had contacted a Finnish contrabandist – he didn't trust the local Russians – one of those who smuggled foodstuffs from Finland to exchange for jewellery and the like with the starving inhabitants of Petrograd. Such men were a rough-and-ready crowd who'd slit your throat for a handful of rubles, Reilly knew that. But at the same time, he told himself, they were very careful, for they knew they'd be shot out of hand as 'foreign reactionaries and economic criminals', if they were caught by the Cheka or the Militia.

Now as midnight approached on this last day of January 1924, he woke the boy and told him to dress, while he prepared himself for the night's journey. The Finn contrabandist, a one-eyed giant named Nikonen, would use his *drovny*, a broad, low sleigh filled with hay, into which he and the boy could snuggle for warmth, drawn by a horse, to take them some twenty miles further up the Finnish frontier, where he had hired a remote country house. It had long been abandoned by the rich middle-class merchant who had once owned it, but the merchant's relatives had been only too happy to accept Reilly's bribe of several pounds of butter and two loaves of black bread for its use. In starving Petrograd such foodstuffs were more precious than gold.

'I can't get anyone to ride a horse in front with a torch,' Nikonen had explained. 'Everyone's so damned jumpy with all these patrols. We'll just have to do it on our own.'

Reilly had nodded his understanding. He knew what the Finn meant. In the old days the man on the horse with the torch had ridden a mile or so in front of the *drovny* in order to ward off the prowling wolves, who were ravenous at this time of year and often chased sledges in pursuit of food.

'No matter. I'm well armed,' Reilly had answered, displaying his two automatics. 'I'm ready for them if they make an appearance.'

The sight had pleased the Finn. He had chuckled, 'And the Cheka as well?'

Reilly had nodded and said laconically, 'Yes. The Cheka, too.'

That had impressed the Finnish contrabandist.

Now as the boy rubbed the sleep out of his eyes and clambered into the peasant clothing which he was still wearing – blouse and breeches, together with a black leather cap – Reilly prepared himself for what was to come. He slipped out the magazines of the two automatics and checked the bright brass slugs. He put two pinches of pepper in his pockets to be used against both man and animal if necessary. He slipped a steel comb into his top pocket. Seemingly harmless, a comb like that, used correctly, could blind a man. And finally he wound around himself the most powerful weapon of all, a money belt filled with the Horsemen of St George.

Now it was midnight. Reilly could hear the hiss of the sledge across the snow. Nikonen was coming to fetch him. He looked at the boy. He was taking this sudden change very calmly. Nothing seemed to upset Serge. It was something that pleased Reilly: he felt it was the sign of aristocratic greatness. The boy would make a good leader of the Russian people … under Reilly's guidance, naturally. 'Come,' he said and extinguished the petroleum lantern. Taking the boy's hand, he went outside.

The *drovny* was pulled up outside, twin jets of grey air coming from the horse's nostrils in the freezing cold. Reilly noted with approval that a couple of inches of fresh snow had fallen. That would suffice to give grip to the horse's hooves.

Nikonen touched his gloved hand to his cap. Reilly helped Serge in and told him to bury himself deep in the sledge's load then he clambered in himself, burying himself in the warming hay next to Serge.

Nikonen cracked his whip and they were off, the runners of the sledge hissing and singing like saws as they headed for the fortress. For Reilly had reasoned that any night patrols of the Cheka or Militia would try to keep out in the open where they had better visibility.

Behind them, over Petrograd, a searchlight swept the skies and then descended to the ground to search it, and Reilly told himself the Reds were on full alert. Obviously things were heading for a crisis now between Stalin and Trotsky. Now the whole military force of the Reds was on duty, preparing for any eventuality. He frowned in his bed of straw. Things were not going as planned. But there was still time. But what if Stalin and Trotsky decide to work together, at least for the time being? an insidious little voice at the back of his brain rasped. What becomes of your plan then?

Reilly frowned at the thought. He knew this was his last chance. He'd never get another opportunity to change the course of world history. Was it possible that the two great rivals might get together and continue to govern Russia as a team? Then all his planning and scheming would come to naught and the boy would be worthless. He looked down at the noble face of the prince sleeping in the straw. What would he do with him then? Already he presented a danger. He was sure by now that the Cheka had learnt of the Romanov boy. Anyone seen with a boy of his age would be suspect. The Chekists or Militiamen would arrest such a person immediately. His frown deepened. He had to be prepared for every contingency.

His reverie was interrupted rudely. '*Gospodin* – citizen!' Nikonen yelled in sudden alarm. 'We're being followed.'

'What!' Reilly swung round hastily.

Coming out from the direction of the village of Lissy now a band of riders, rifles bouncing up and down over their shoulders, were urging on their horses with their whips. 'Militia!' Reilly cried in alarm, recognizing the riders immediately. He turned to the driver. 'Ten thousand Finnish marks if you get away!' he cried.

The Finn needed no urging. He knew his own life as a contrabandist was forfeit if he were captured. He lashed his whip over the back of the pony and it broke into a gallop. The sledge leapt forward.

Reilly pulled the twin automatics from his pocket. Beside him, unaware of what was happening, the boy slept on. Now the chase commenced. The Finn lashed and thrashed the pony's glistening flank. The sledge flew across the ice and snow. But the riders kept pace. Indeed now an anxious Reilly could see they were gaining, but they were still out of pistol range. A carbine slug hit the snow a few metres behind the flying sledge. Reilly cursed. His automatic was no match at that range for the rider's carbine. Their only chance was the forest. 'Head for the trees, man!' he yelled above the hiss of the runners, as the riders fired again and a little angry flurry of snow erupted close to the sledge.

Nikonen lashed the horse's glistening rump and tugged the reins to the right, shouting at the animal in Finnish. The trees loomed ever closer. Reilly prayed they would reach them in time. In the forest the riders would have to break up and slow down. Then, if necessary, he'd tackle them with his two automatics. It wouldn't be the first time he had been forced to shoot himself out of an impossible situation.

Now they were perhaps only a hundred metres or so from the edge of the fir forest. The riders, realising what the sledge driver was about, split up into two groups. Crouched low over the flying manes of their mounts, they dug their spurs cruelly into the horses' sides, as they raced forward in two horns, attempting to cut off the sledge before it reached the cover of the trees.

'Come on, man!' Reilly yelled frantically above the hiss of the sleds and the crackle of carbine fire. *Twenty* thousand marks if you get us out of this!' It would be a small fortune to the Finnish smuggler, but it would be worth it to escape with a whole hide.

Furiously the Finn lashed the rump of his flying pony. Left and right the leather reins struck its flesh. The pony put all it had into the flight, hooves flying across the snow. But still the pursuers were gaining on them.

Suddenly, frighteningly, disaster struck. The right runner hit a hidden obstacle, perhaps a rock jutting out of the ice. It splintered with a sharp crack. Next instant the sledge had overturned to the right, throwing the two in the hay to the left, while the driver remained trapped on his perch.

The boy awoke with a start. Reilly clasped his hand across the boy's mouth so that he didn't cry out. 'Quick,' he hissed, 'follow me.' Then the two of them were running in the darkness, followed by the thunder of the horses' hooves and the curses of the trapped Finnish driver.

Reilly flung a glance over his shoulder as they pelted for the cover of the trees. The riders had halted and were swinging down from their horses. He guessed why. They presumed they had trapped a smuggler. Whatever he was carrying, they would loot. Once they found there was nothing, they would resume the chase. He had to get himself and the boy into the cover of the trees while there was still time.

Behind him the riders had righted the sledge and freed the trapped driver. He could hear their shouted questions carried to him by the wind. He could hear the Finn declaring in broken Russian, '*Ya na znayu* –

I don't know.' That was followed by the sound of a slap. Someone shouted angrily, '*Nichtevo* – nothing.' They had discovered that there was nothing to be looted. In a moment they would find out that the Finn had been carrying passengers and not smuggled goods.

Desperately the two of them stumbled forward over the ice, grey and black in the starry light of the stars. Ahead of them the windswept paths leading to the forest looked like black pits.

Reilly had a sudden idea. Already behind him he could hear the jingle of bits and the rattle of equipment as the riders remounted their horses. They'd never make the forest now. 'Get down, boy,' he commanded urgently. 'Over there in that patch of black ice – not the grey. *Quick!* Here they come.'

Puzzled, the boy did as he was commanded, as the clatter of the horses' hooves came ever nearer.

Reilly held his breath. He prayed his scheme would work. He knew he had never been as close to death as this. Now he could hear the squeaking of the ice groaning under the weight of men and horses. They were very close. But he daren't look up. Would they do as he anticipated? He lay there tense, nerves ticking electrically with suspense.

But the riders, carefully picking their way forward, did do as he anticipated. They chose the grey spots and not the black area, slick with ice. They knew if their mount went down it might well result in a broken leg and they didn't want that at this late time of the night in this remote place.

He waited, feeling the icy cold seep into his body. He dare not move. Behind him the Finn wailed as they hit him again. Now the riders were returning. Reilly gripped the boy's hand hard and willed him not to move, not to cry out.

Again the ice vibrated under the weight of the riders. He knew he could have reached out and touched one of them; they were that close. God, he hoped one of them didn't ride over him!

And then they were past. Moments later he heard the hiss of the sledge leaving with them. Slowly, very slowly, Reilly rose, first on all fours so as to present the smallest possible outline, then standing finally upright. The riders and the sledge were gone. Above the stars twinkled, as if to say, A narrow squeak. But a miss is as good as a mile. Sidney Reilly's proverbial luck had held again. But even as he told himself that, he knew with a sense of growing despair that his grand plan had failed. Soon the Cheka would know everything.

Chapter Four

Aronson tossed the *Pravda* on to his desk with a grunted, 'So they've patched up their quarrel for the time being. Our new masters are to be Trotsky and Stalin.' He pulled one of the long *paparoki* from its box, lit it, and breathed out a stream of blue smoke.

'What do you think?' Ilona asked curiously.

'It won't last,' he said after a moment's thought. 'Both of them want to be the sole master of Russia. But for the time being the crisis is over. There'll be peace.'

It was the beautiful blonde's turn to frown. 'Will we never be rid of the rats?' she asked.

'One day,' he answered with a cold smile, telling himself that his colleagues of the Cheka would hit the ceiling if they could hear what she was calling them right in the middle of their own headquarters. 'Communism won't – can't – work. But God only knows when the whole system will fall apart. Perhaps not in our lifetime.'

'I hope you're wrong, darling.'

'I hope so. But our main concern is Russia – how to save our mother country.' His jaw hardened. 'Whatever the system, Mother Russia must be our first priority.'

She nodded and said, 'We have suffered so much, we Russians. We deserve better than this – this corruption, starvation, systematic murder–'

He held up his hand to stop her speaking any more. 'Yes, I agree. But enough of that kind of talk. It is too hard a burden for me to bear when I think of all those injustices you have named.'

'All right, darling, what of this man Reilly and the Romanov?'

'Well, at first the Finn was truculent. He knew we were going to shoot him, so why tell us anything?' Aronson answered her question. 'The Finns are, by nature, a damned stubborn race. But we worked on him all right.' He smiled coldly at the memory of what had happened in the cellars two hours before.

It had been a very simple and indeed

primitive form of torture. No pulling out of teeth one by one or electrodes attached to the nipples and genitals for the electric shock treatment. They had simply placed an old tin pail over the bound Finn's head and whacked it with the slops brush. With each whack, gobs of blood had shot from beneath onto the white-tiled floor. By the time they had finished, the Finn had blood pouring from his nose, ears and mouth and he was so dazed he could hardly focus his eyes.

His speech blurred, voice high-pitched and almost feminine, as if he had been castrated, he had told them what he knew. Aronson had made him go through his statement twice. He wanted to have the descriptions of the two people that the contrabandist had been carrying, exactly. 'Medium-sized ... dark ... looked like a Yid,' the Finn had stuttered, coughing up blood all the time. 'Lots of money... English gold money.'

'It was Reilly and this supposed Romanov heir all right,' Aronson told Ilona now. 'Beyond all doubt. And they got away.' He stroked his chin thoughtfully.

Outside in the courtyard, the officer commanding the firing squad was bellowing, 'Firing party – *take aim!*'

'Now Reilly and the boy are on the run in

the depth of winter. He undoubtedly has plenty of those Horsemen of St George of the English to bribe his way to freedom. But every frontier guard in the province has been warned to be on the lookout for a man and a boy. The boy will be his downfall and Reilly knows that. Alone, he might well escape.' Aronson shrugged slightly. 'After all, he has managed to survive as an agent and troublemaker for thirty years. But with the boy I don't think he has a chance.'

'What will he do then?' Ilona asked.

Again Aronson shrugged.

From outside there came the clicking of a dozen rifle bolts being drawn back. 'Party,' the officer in charge bellowed, *'fire!'*

There was the crash of musketry. Ilona started. A shriek of pain. Then a long echoing silence.

Aronson looked at his nails. Executions took place at the Cheka HQ all the time, but he still could never get used to them. A man – or woman for that matter – was alive one moment, dead the next.

Ilona licked suddenly dry lips and said, 'You were saying, darling?'

'Oh yes, about Reilly,' he answered. 'With the boy he doesn't stand a chance, with all the money in the world to pay bribes, grease palms… Without him, he does.'

'Do you mean,' she said in a hushed voice, 'that he'll get rid of the boy?… Get rid of a Romanov?' She loomed at him, eyes full of fear.

He nodded.

'But you can't let him kill a Romanov – the last of the Romanovs!' she cried. 'Haven't they suffered enough? No,' she pleaded with him, her beautiful face contorted with shock and horror. *'You must do something!'*

He reached out a hand and took hers in his. 'Calm yourself, Ilona,' he said soothingly. 'But you must realise that I am virtually powerless. Reilly is somewhere out there in the wastes along the Finnish frontier. We'd need an army to patrol that area correctly and you know how feckless our people are, especially in the depth of winter…' He saw the look in her green eyes and added hastily, 'I'll try my best, Ilona. Honestly. If I can I won't let any harm come to that little boy…'

A hundred miles away on the other side of the Finnish frontier, 'Finnegans" locomotive had rumbled to a halt. Again they had run out of logs for the boiler. Now the crew of the *Swordfish*, save for Billy Bennett and Ginger Kerrigan who were on watch, were busy sawing logs in the nearby forest. Both the officers helped, for they knew they had to make the coast before nightfall. On the morrow they'd reassemble the *Swordfish*, ready for the rescue operation.

The air was so cold that their eyebrows hung heavy with hoarfrost and their breath, as they hacked and sawed at the firs along the track, wreathed up around them in a grey cloud. Still, all of them were happy. Soon they knew they'd be taking the fugitives back to Britain, and as Ginger put it, 'There'll be real wallop and tarts – lovely grub,' to which Billy added, 'Ay, and egg and chips. Proper scoff. None of this here raw fish stuff these foreigners eat.'

It was about noon when Ginger, perched behind the Lewis gun on the flat car, spotted the riders. About a mile to their front, silent black specks were moving across the frozen snow which glittered like a myriad diamonds in the weak yellow rays of the winter sun. They were heading towards the narrow cutting they would have to pass on their way to the coast.

'What do you think, Ginger?' Billy asked in that ponderous manner of his.

'Get a butcher's of him,' Ginger replied. He indicated one of the riders who had dismounted and was approaching the railway cutting, crouched and cautious. 'Yer don't move like that if you've nuthin' to frigging hide.'

'Ay, yer right there, Ginger.'

'I'm allus frigging right, matey,' Ginger replied. 'Yer better tell Mr Smith – toot-sweet.'

Minutes later Bird and Smith were survey-ing the mysterious riders through their binoculars. 'They're armed all right,' Dickie Bird said, lowering his glasses.

'And they're not wearing any kind of uni-form either,' Smith said. 'So we can con-clude from that that they are–'

'Those damned Red bandits,' Mrs Reilly cut into their conversation decisively. 'It's obvious that they are after us and we know who put them up to it – and the station-master.'

'You mean Moscow?' Smith said, looking up at her glowing cheeks and fine sparkling dark eyes.

She nodded.

Dickie Bird said, 'You can see their plan. They must have ridden hell-for-leather across-country when we did a bunk from that station, in an attempt to cut us off up there at the pass.

'Not an *attempt*, Dickie,' Smith said grimly. 'They have cut us off, to my way of thinking. I doubt if Finnegan's old engine could do more than ten miles an hour up that incline. A couple of hand grenades tossed down at us from the top of the cutting and our hash would be settled for good, I'm afraid.' Suddenly Smith was aware of Mrs Reilly's hand creeping into his. He turned and stared at her. She was afraid for the first time since he had known her. He guessed what she was thinking. If she fell into the bandits' hands alive, they'd do more than just rob her. He forced a smile. 'Come on, you lot, don't look like a wet weekend in Wigan. We'll outfox 'em yet, I'll be bound.'

'Ay, ye're right, sir,' Ferguson snarled, his wrinkled face set in a look of boundless contempt. 'I mind they're only a bunch o' foreigners.' He spat contemptuously over this side of the cab. 'They're nae match for the lads of the old Royal.'

'Well said, Chiefie,' Dickie Bird agreed enthusiastically. 'I bet you told jolly old Nelson the same at Trafalgar.'

Ferguson glowered at the young officer but said nothing.

'Now, I guess they haven't seen us yet,' Smith said thoughtfully. 'They'll have heard us, I'm sure, but not seen us, due to the forest on both sides of the line. So they'll be waiting for us to come up the line and then get on with their dirty business. Now what if we did this…?'

The ancient locomotive started to puff and pant its way up the steep slope. In their hiding places to both sides of the cutting, the Red bandits tensed, weapons at the ready, grenades piled up in front of them on the snow. Belching black smoke, the engine slowed down, its wheels clattering on the icy tracks, sending up flurries of blue-red sparks.

The bandit leader, a great hulking fellow with shifty eyes, surveyed the slow-moving train. Obviously the men on the train suspected nothing. He could see the dark outlines of the passengers in the single coach slumped forward as if they were asleep while at the front the engine driver was busily tossing logs into the firebox in order to keep up the steam pressure. He raised his right arm and waited, counting off the distance to himself as the train chugged ever closer. *Three hundred metres … two fifty … two hundred metres … one hundred and fifty…* Crouched in their hiding places at the top of the cutting the bandits started to pull the pins from their hand grenades… *'One hundred metres…'* The bandit leader began to bring his arm down slowly. Already his mind was full of the reward this attack would bring him from Petrograd and the loot there was bound to be on the train. There was a woman too. He licked his thick cracked lips at the thought. He hadn't had a woman for a week. It would give him the greatest of pleasure to make her spread her legs. He could visualize it already. *Fifty metres…*

'Now!' the bandit leader cried in the very same instant that the Lewis gun to their rear opened up with a vicious burst of fire.

He screamed with pain as his back was ripped open. The grenade dropped from his suddenly lifeless fingers to explode at his feet. Slowly, his severed head began to trundle down the hill.

Now Ginger and Billy Bennett sprayed the whole area with their slugs. There was no escape from that cruel fire. Men went down everywhere. One of the bandits, wounded in both legs, attempted to crawl towards the machine gunners, grenade in his right hand. They didn't give him a chance. 'Try this one on for size, you bolshy git!' Ginger snarled and gave him a burst. His upturned face melted downwards like hot red sealing wax.

In the end it wasn't war; it was a massacre...

The survivors fled, followed by that deadly fire, jostling and shouting angrily at each other in their panic-stricken attempt to reach their horses and escape. Only five did so. The rest remained where they lay in the bloody snow, dead or dying, food for the wolves once night fell.

Half an hour later they were on their way again, weary but happy at the way the trick had worked out. Behind them the dead Reds stiffened in the cold.

Chapter Five

Forty-eight hours later they had reassembled the *Swordfish* at Virojoki, a small harbour, within sight of the Russian frontier and overlooking the strait which led to Petrograd itself. For the first twenty-four hours after their arrival, while the crew worked all out to get the vessel into shape, Smith was worried that during their long and adventurous passage to this remote place, some damage could have been done to the *Swordfish's* internal workings. But a quick sea trial had assured him. The Thorneycroft engines had worked perfectly and all the control equipment seemed to be behaving normally. As CPO Ferguson had said proudly, patting the *Swordfish's* hull as if she were some pet dog, 'Ye canna beat the old *Swordfish*. Yon's a tough old bird, I'll be minding.' To which Dickie Bird had replied cheekily, 'Not surprised. After all she was built by the English and not some remote place on the Clyde.'

Now after all the excitements of the voyage from Hull and the tension and worry for the last forty-eight hours, a kind of bored stalemate set in. The port was a small place, perhaps a couple of thousand inhabitants, none of whom seemed to speak English save 'Finnegan' who had decided, for some reason known only to himself, to stay with them.

'Ye'll nae gang to them knocking-shops and rum-houses,' Ferguson had warned the crew sternly. 'Any man getting the pox and I'll have ye on a fizzer for a self-inflicted wound.'

'I'd like to see the tart's wound first,' Ginger had ventured boldly, while Billy Bennett had moaned, 'Can't we go and get us some scoff, Chiefie? I'm sick of the old bully.'

'Nothing wrong with corned beef, mon.'

Ferguson had rounded upon him. 'Better than all that foreign muck.'

But in the end he had relented and, with Smith's permission, had allowed the crew to go and see the sights. 'But ye mind ye go in twos. I'm nae having yer getting yer silly heads knocked off by the locals. Ye never know with them foreigners,' he added darkly.

So while the men wandered off to enjoy themselves the best they could in the snow-shrouded little town perched on the edge of the fiord, Smith and Dickie Bird waited, bored, in the *Swordfish's* tiny wardroom, sipping pink gin and smoking moodily.

Mrs Reilly had gone into the town accompanied by Finnegan as an interpreter in case she met someone who didn't understand her Russian.

'You like her, Smithie,' Dickie Bird said, looking up from an ancient copy of *Punch*.

'What?'

'Mrs Reilly, you like her.'

Smith looked across at his old friend, whom he'd known ever since they had both gone to Harrow-on-the-Hill at the age of thirteen. He knew that Dickie knew. So he said, 'I've been to bed with her.'

'I thought so,' Dickie said carefully, as if he

didn't want to embarrass his friend with his usual flippant manner. 'What are you going to do about it?'

Smith considered for a few moments. Outside it had begun to snow once more. Soft, sad flakes drifting down out of a grey sky. 'There's nothing much I can do about it,' he said after a while. 'Help her to get her husband and the boy out. Then that's that.' He made a gesture of cleaning one hand off against another.

'All for the best, I suppose, Smithie, old bean. There's not much that sailor chaps like us can expect but a tumble in the hay with a willing little filly and then bob's your uncle.'

'You have a gift with words, old chap,' Smith said and laughed, relieved now that Dickie Bird knew. They had known each other too long and had been through too many things together to have secrets from one another. 'But she's a fine woman, Dickie, don't think I don't see her good qualities under that tough exterior of hers. I want things to go well for her.'

'And so they shall, Smithie,' Dickie said with forced enthusiasm. 'Now before you start contemplating the jolly old navel, what about wrapping yourself around a large pink gin?' He swung his legs down from the battered leather stool.

'You're a good fellow, Dickie,' Smith said enthusiastically.

Lightly Dickie said, quoting the old quip of the Great War, 'Some say dear old Sarnt major. Other buggers tell the truth.' He reached for the bottle of Booth's pink gin.

A mile away, Mrs Reilly stared at the little runt of a man in his shabby clothes, with eyes that refused to meet her own. 'Say that again, *gospodin?*' she said, voice hard and demanding.

The man standing in front of her, shifting his black leather cap round nervously in his hands held in front of his skinny stomach, quavered, 'It's not wise to talk about these things too openly madam. But as I have just said, The Petrograd Cheka know about your husband and the Romanov boy. They have put out a number one priority alert with the details of the two of them. They emphasize looking for a man of your husband's appearance accompanied by a boy. A picture of your husband is going to be posted everywhere. He hasn't a chance of surviving if he doesn't get out within the next twenty-four hours.'

Mrs Reilly's brain raced. She knew her husband and she knew that he *did* have a chance of getting out of Russia, but that it would require he did the unthinkable.

She knew nothing of the boy save that he was supposed to be the last surviving Romanov. But he *was* a mere child! How could she allow Sidney to murder him or abandon him to the Russian winter, which her husband would undoubtedly do? Always it had been her husband's first priority to save his own skin – something he had done remarkably well over the last thirty years. No, the boy was as good as dead, if she didn't do something and do it soon.

It was then that the landlord of the little local inn at which she was staying for the sake of propriety – she would have dearly loved to have slept with the handsome young English officer again this night – had jumped at the knock on the door of her bedroom. The little runt looked frightened, but when she called 'Come in' in Russian, it was only the little engine driver Finnegan.

He bowed with exaggerated politeness and said, 'Madam, there is another messenger outside for you.'

'*Another?* Show him up at once,' she ordered.

Finnegan grinned. 'Can't, madam. The owner of the inn won't let him in the place. He says he smell too great.' His grin broadened. 'He is a Lapp,' he added as if that explained everything. 'Look.' He pointed at the window.

Through it she could see a dark-faced man standing next to a reindeer sledge. He was dressed in home-tanned skins with strange skin shoes on his feet, complete with tassels. Even at that distance he didn't look as if he washed very often and she recollected suddenly that in winter the nomadic Lapps rubbed their faces with animal fat to keep out the cold and frost. 'What was his message?' she asked Finnegan.

Hastily Finnegan took the scrap of paper from his pocket and handed it to her. With fingers that trembled slightly she opened it and read the obviously hastily pencilled message. *'Tight spot. Must leave here almost at once. Now on the frontier road from Suurpaala to Vaalimaa. The Lapp knows position. Help expected – need. Love S.R.'*

She flushed, a little angry. It was typical Sidney – *'Help expected – need.'* He loved to give orders, but she had no time to dwell on that now. Hastily she sought her purse, and handed the little runt five sovereigns. He raised his cap, said, 'Thank you, Gracious Lady', and was off as quickly as his bow legs would carry him.

She turned to Finnegan. 'Bring that Lapp. We must get to the boat immediately.'

Finnegan grinned all over his ugly face. 'Lapp, he don't like city. Scared. But I'll make him come.' He tapped the revolver which bulged in his right pocket. 'He come OK.'

She grinned back at the little engine driver. Nothing seemed to perturb him. Indeed she felt he was really enjoying his time spent with the *Swordfish* crew, despite the dangers. A few minutes later, to the astonishment of the innkeeper, the three of them walked out of the door.

Half an hour later, the whole crew of the *Swordfish* were crowded into the ship's tiny wardroom, while outside Finnegan guarded the Lapp and his mangy reindeer to ensure they didn't run away. Briefly, Mrs Reilly told them what she knew and that her husband needed help urgently to get out of Russia. But for the time being she didn't tell them about her fears for the boy.

They listened attentively until she had finished, when Smith said briskly, 'Let's have a look at the chart.' Swiftly the chart of the part of the Baltic they were currently in was produced, laid out on the wardroom table and secured with two inkwells. 'Here's Suurpaala, where the Lapp left. Here! And here, Vaalimaa, the nearest Finnish town, just on the other side of the border.' He sniffed and stared hard at the chart before saying, 'Now, the fiord where we are now runs up to just perhaps half a mile below the Finnish town. If we could get them both across the frontier and if the Russians don't attempt to block the exit from the fiord, we could be out on the open sea within the hour.'

Now it was Dickie Bird's turn to sniff. 'Seems like a deuced lot of "if's" to me, old boy,' he said slowly.

'I know, Dickie. But it's the only kind of plan I can think of in a hurry.' He looked around the crowded, smoke-filled ward-room. 'What do you chaps think? After all, you're going to risk your necks as well.'

CPO Ferguson glared around the faces of the crew, threateningly, as if daring any one of them to object. He need not have feared. For there was a mumbled, 'We're with you, sir,' from most of them.

'Thank you, chaps,' Smith said, genuinely

moved. 'I knew I could rely on you. I always can.'

'But how are we going to let Mr Reilly know what the rendezvous is going to be?' Dickie asked. 'We can hardly rely on that chap outside with that moose of his or whatever the dreadful-looking creature is.'

'I shall go,' Mrs Reilly said hastily, thinking of the boy. Time was running out if she were to save him.

Smith looked at her, his mind racing. He remembered what C had told him. That on no account should he cross the Russian frontier. But he knew he couldn't let her go alone. 'I shall go with you. We'll take Finnegan, too. He knows the lingo,' he said quietly.

Dickie Bird looked shocked. 'Remember what C said, Smithie?' he said. 'There's a price on your head – on *all* our heads.'

'I know. That's why I am going alone. We're all at risk as it is, being so close to the Russian frontier. I wouldn't put it past them to cross the frontier if they thought there was a chance of harming us. Not much the tiny Finnish army could do about it either. Now then,' he went on urgently, as it appeared that Dickie Bird might object, 'let's get this thing on the road...'

Two hours later the *Swordfish* sailed. Already it was dark and Dickie Bird had ordered that just one riding light would be switched on. He wanted their departure to be as discreet as possible. Slowly, almost noiselessly, with the Thorneycroft engines purring softly, they started to enter deeper into the fiord. The men were tense. There was none of the usual joking and laughing which went with most new departures. For even the dullest of the crew knew the risk they were running, only a couple of miles from the Russian frontier; and the even greater risk that Lieutenant Smith was taking with the woman. All of them carried revolvers, and Ginger Kerrigan had rigged up the Lewis gun just behind the bridge with the silent approval of CPO Ferguson, his craggy old face set in a worried look at the thought of the risks Mr Smith was taking.

On the shore, watching them go, the cross-eyed little runt who had told Mrs Reilly that her husband was wanted, sucked his dingy teeth thoughtfully for a while until the *Swordfish* disappeared into the velvet darkness. Then he turned and began to crunch his way back over the frozen snow to the little inn. The call to Petrograd would be a long, complicated and expensive business,

247

but in the end it might well turn out very profitable indeed. He smiled crookedly at the thought of a week in one of those gypsy brothels in Petrograd, with as many women as he wanted and vodka too. Yes, he told himself, comrade Aronson knew just how well to reward informers...

Chapter Six

Aronson flashed Ilona a look of triumph, as he placed the phone down. It was midnight and he had been in bed with Ilona on the office couch when the phone had rung. Now he was wide awake and buzzing with energy. He told her quickly what his inform-ant on the other side of the Gulf in Finland had just told him and said, 'So now we can virtually pin down Reilly's position.' He looked down at her naked body but his eyes did not take in those splendid full breasts with their great, dark brown nipples or the spread legs with a hint of pink flesh showing in the dark triangle of pubic hair. His eyes were on other things: Reilly captured at last, being brought into his office in chains.

'After thirty years of working and plotting against our Mother Russia, we've got him,' he said eagerly, mind racing electrically.

'What will you do?' she asked, pouting a little, for the phone call had interrupted their lovemaking just when she had been about to climax, carried away by an almost uncontrollable, wild passion. Now she could see that the magnificent erection which had stuck out like a policeman's club before he had mounted her was beginning to diminish rapidly.

'Flood the area with the troops, frontier police and my own men immediately,' he said. 'We'll fine-toothcomb the whole place. But I shall ensure that even if Reilly does get away, we'll get him in the end.' Naked still, he strode across to the huge map of Northern Russia which covered one wall of his office and looked at it thoughtfully while she gazed at his naked torso. What a beautiful body he had, she told herself: broad-shouldered and narrow-waisted. Aronson radiated sheer animal strength. She felt the thrill of desire flood her own body once more and she shivered with delightful anticipation.

'One of our submarines from the Red Fleet at Kronstadt could make it to the entrance of the fiord at Vitolathi,' he mused aloud, rubbing his jaw as he did so. 'If Reilly does make it, he'll be coming out in that boat of those two damned English adventurers and bandits. A sub, positioned at the straits there, and they wouldn't have a chance.'

'Come back to the couch,' she pleaded, 'you'll catch cold.'

He turned and looked at her sternly. Then his stern look gave way to a smile. 'Yes, you are right. I will come back to bed for a little while. We – you and I – deserve some pleasure before it all starts, eh?'

She giggled with delight as he slid in beside her and she felt his firm, muscular hardness once more. Her hand fell to his soft organ. She took it and directed it between her legs. Gently she rubbed it against her clitoris. Over and over again, her own breath coming in short, excited gasps. He looked at her white hand as he did so. He thought how beautiful it looked, as if she were holding a flower. For a while he contained himself to see what Ilona would do. He willed himself not to harden and watched as beads of moisture started to appear at the entrance to the pink slit. It was exciting, very exciting.

'Put your tongue in my mouth,' she gasped huskily. 'Please!'

Aronson did as she commanded. Now

each time his penis touched her slit, she touched the tip of his tongue with hers. It seemed to Aronson that a delightful warmth ran from his tongue to his penis and then back again as she did so.

'Stick your tongue out,' she commanded, her voice suddenly very harsh. *'Out – now!'*

She took the tongue in her mouth, sucking it intensely. He felt himself harden in spite of himself. He broke out in a sweat. She parted her legs and began rubbing him with two slender fingers. Now he was panting like a dog, wanting to penetrate her, thrust himself violently into her body. Then he could contain himself no longer. He pushed her hand away. With a savage grunt he thrust himself into that delightful burning moist hole.

Thus they writhed and bucked, grunting obscenities, thrusting at each other as if they wanted to hurt the other person, bodies lathered in sweat, gasping for breath, the world forgotten, concerned only with their own savage pleasures…

But later while they lay side by side, smoking and staring at the ceiling, content, happy, wordless, Aronson knew that this night the fate of Mother Russia had been decided for a little while. The Romanov threat was over…

It was bitterly cold and there were flurries of snow in the air. But the three sturdy little ponies pulling the *troika* struggled on bravely, steam jetting from their nostrils as they exerted all their strength. The Horsemen of St George had played their habitual, useful role at the first village he and the boy had come to after their escape. The *apparatchik*, running the state-owned lumberyard there, had looked at the two fugitives curiously and Reilly had reached for the comforting, hard feel of his automatic in his pocket. But the *apparatchik* had asked no questions. He had given them glasses of hot tea, followed by a meal of black bread and hunks of cured bacon before having the horses and the *troika* sledge brought from the stables. Reilly had told himself both were the property of the state, but such things never worried *apparatchiks;* they ran state-owned institutions for their own benefit. An hour later they had set off again with Reilly on the cab. He had taken the direction leading back to Petrograd just in case the *apparatchik* was watching. Then when the village was out of sight, he had circled back and round it through the forest and continued his progress westwards to the frontier.

That had been six hours ago. Now he knew he couldn't be more than five miles away from the frontier and the point of rendezvous with the Lapp who had taken his message to Finland, was less than two miles off. Once he reached it, he'd find some sort of cover for the rest of the night, till dawn.

But what if the Lapp doesn't turn up again? a harsh little voice at the back of his mind rasped. *Or if he's late and the frontier area is swarming with police?* He knew the nomadic Lapps were notoriously careless about time. Their year wasn't divided into months, weeks, hours. They divided a year into two seasons. The summer when they trekked north in search of forage for their animals and the winter when they came south for the same purpose. What would they know of clocks and time?

Reilly flung a glance over his shoulder at the boy sleeping in the straw, only his face showing. He bit his bottom lip. He told himself that if the Lapp didn't turn up to lead the two of them through the frontier posts to safety in Finland then the boy had to go. Without him and with the help of those golden Horsemen of the Bank of England he stood a fighting chance of getting through.

In essence, the boy's fate would be decided in the next twenty-four hours. He turned and cracked his whip across the backs of the three ponies. They struggled on through the freezing night. Behind, in the hay, the last of the Romanovs slept on, unaware of the great danger he was in, the sleeping face revealing only innocence and trust...

At a much slower pace the two sledges pulled by the dour Lapp's reindeer moved eastwards towards that same frontier. According to Finnegan, their guide barely spoke Finnish and no Russian at all, save 'papiroki' – 'cigarette'. So much of the communication with him had to be made in a crude kind of sign language. But all their attempts in Finnish and in sign language had failed to make him move faster. As Finnegan said, 'These Lapps know only two speeds, gentlemens – slow and dead slow.' And he hadn't laughed at the joke.

Thus Mrs Reilly and Smith huddled in the first sledge, packed with hay, while Finnegan brought up the rear in the second one; and by now the two lovers knew why. The smell which came from the Lapp, directly in front of them guiding the reindeer, was horrific. 'I swear he hasn't been washed since the day he was born,' Smith said, nauseated by the stench of unwashed body, mouldy skins and the coarse black Russian *morhoka* tobacco, which their guide smoked.

Still, the man knew the way all right. He plodded on unerringly, and Smith, who was navigating by means of the stars whenever the snow flurries didn't obscure the night sky, could see he was proceeding steadily southeast. What kind of navigation the Lapp used, he didn't know – there were few landmarks visible as far as he could see – but the Lapp was taking them ever closer to that dreaded Russo-Finnish frontier that C had warned them never to cross.

Instinctively he reached into the pocket of his old navy jacket to feel if his automatic was still there. She felt the movement and touched his hand gently. 'You are so brave and kind, risking your life like this.'

'It was the least I could after – you know what,' he replied.

'I'm glad you did so, de Vere, because there is another thing–' She hesitated.

He prompted her with, 'Go on, tell me.'

She told him what she feared Reilly would do to the boy if they didn't reach him in time and stop him. He gasped with shock and snorted, 'But surely he wouldn't do anything like that!'

She nodded sadly. 'He would,' she said simply.

'Then we must reach them before the others do. How can anyone kill a harmless boy just to save his own skin? Why, he could surrender the little chap to the Red authorities and we could make such a stink in the West that they wouldn't dare to harm a single hair on his head. These days the Reds need to trade with us, not like back in 1918. They need our good will.'

'But they don't need Sidney Reilly. He's been a long-term thorn in their flesh,' she replied. 'They'd torture all his secrets out of him and then they'd put him up against a wall and shoot him out of hand. No,' she concluded, 'Sidney Reilly is out for number one. He'd never approach the Soviet authorities.'

Silently Smith absorbed the information, as they ploughed through the snow steadily eastwards. By now, he told himself, the *Swordfish* would be in position and waiting. He could guess just how anxiously Dickie Bird and the rest of the crew would be waiting for their reappearance. God, how he wished he had them with him at this moment. They would have been just the kind of backing he might well need, especially now as it was clear that this Reilly fellow was a killer, out to save his own skin, who probably didn't give a damn about his wife and certainly wouldn't risk his life for others.

'It's all right,' he broke the heavy silence, voice full of reassurance, 'we're going to do it. We've *got* to do it. We must save that boy – and damn Reilly!'

'Damn Reilly!' she said with equal vehemence.

Then they both lapsed into silence, each of them wrapped in a cocoon of his own thoughts and apprehensions.

About three in the morning, the two of them awoke from an uneasy dose to find Finnegan bending over them. His breath smelt of vodka and garlic. But they had no time to comment on the fact for he whispered urgently, 'River Sestro.'

Smith woke up within seconds. The Sestro marked the frontier between Finland and Russia. He sat up. He looked urgently to left and right. To his left there were the dark outlines of several wooden houses, their roofs heavy with snow. That would probably be the barracks for the Finnish frontier guards, he told himself. To his right was a little wooden bridge. Under the yellow light of a storm lantern hung up on the Finnish end there was a Finnish sentry, his bayonet gleaming in the light. There was darkness on the Soviet side some twenty paces away. But Smith guessed there would be a similar sentry there. 'What's the drill?' Smith whispered.

'Gentlemens,' Finnegan whispered back, 'we go to the right. There are woods there. The Lapp he say, water not deep so you can—' He searched for the word.

'—Ford it,' Mrs Reilly supplied the words he needed.

'Yes, ford it.' Finnegan grinned in the darkness, showing his mouthful of rotten teeth and Smith turned his head sharply as he caught a whiff of that garlic-laden breath.

'Come on then, let's go,' Smith urged and got out of the sledge. She did the same without being asked. She knew he wanted the sledge lightened for the water. She knew, too, that he wanted to be on his feet and able to move fast in case there was any trouble. They set off again.

Carefully, very carefully, watching that they didn't knock the deep snow off the skeletal branches of the trees, they descended to the river. Smith could hear the gurgling of water so he concluded the Sestro had not frozen over. They descended the steep bank under cover of the trees.

Now they could see the silver sheen of the river in the hard, cold light of the stars. Beyond, the opposite bank seemed deserted. Showing no emotion whatsoever, the Lapp led the first sledge into the water. It bucked and tossed on the little wavelets, but kept its place. A moment later he, Mrs Reilly and Finnegan followed with the second sledge. The bone-chilling cold of the water ate right into their flesh immediately. Mrs Reilly's teeth started to chatter. Smith told himself he was not far off doing the same.

Doggedly they pressed on. To Smith's ears they seemed to be making a devil of a noise splashing across. But the dark shapes of the two sentries on the other side didn't move. They might have been dead, for all he knew.

The first reindeer splashed on to the opposite bank. A moment later Smith and Mrs Reilly followed with their sledge. Smith told himself that for the first time in his life he was on Russian soil, in the land of the enemy where his life was forfeit if he were captured. He dismissed that worrying thought immediately. Together with the Finn, he started to help drag the sledge up the steep bank, praying that the noise the reindeer was making as it blundered and puffed up the

259

slope, wouldn't be heard.

But now their luck ran out.

Suddenly – startlingly – a flashlight was turned on. Its beam, hard and white, cutting the velvet darkness, swung their way and came to rest on the Lapp standing there holding the reindeer's halter.

'*Stoi?*' a harsh voice demanded in Russian.

For a moment they stood there as if frozen for eternity, then Smith shouted urgently, 'Run for it!' and they were blundering, man and animal, through the forest as the first wild firing broke out.

Chapter Seven

Frantically Reilly lashed the steaming backs of the ponies. 'Go faster you devils!' he yelled at them in English above the hiss of the *troika's* runners. Behind him the boy woke with a start. He levered himself out of the straw. 'What's the matter, Uncle?'

Reilly didn't reply. He couldn't. He was too busy handling the ponies as they galloped over the frozen surface of the new snow. The whole frontier area seemed to have exploded into action. Red and green signal flares were sailing into the night sky on all sides. From far away he could hear shouts, commands, curses. Somewhere an ancient machine gun was ticking away like an irate woodpecker and he was sure he could hear the faint clatter of cavalry accoutrements behind him.

He careened around a corner of the forest trail, the sledge momentarily balancing on one runner. Four militiamen stood there, one of them holding a red lantern in his hand. All had their rifles slung. Reilly freed one hand from the reins, placing the lead in between his teeth as he had seen the Cossacks do in the charge. His automatic appeared as if by magic in the free hand. Frantically the militiamen tried to unsling their carbines. Reilly beat them to it. His automatic spat scarlet flame. The militiaman with the red lantern spun round with a scream of agony. Next moment the lantern fell from his suddenly lifeless fingers and shattered on the ground. Next to him another cop slammed against a tree as if propelled there by a giant fist. Slowly he slithered down the trunk, leaving a trail of red behind him. A moment later Reilly was through, his body trembling with shock.

'*Horosho* … good, Uncle!' the boy chortled, as he held on to the sides of the dangerously swaying sledge. 'You showed them!'

But Reilly knew he wasn't out of danger yet. His shooting would have already attracted more attention from the Reds. He was sure that he could hear the clatter of cavalry behind him once more. They'd head for the site of the shooting and then they'd take up the pursuit in earnest.

But Reilly was wrong. The cavalry wasn't behind him. It was to his front. He turned another bend in the trail and there they were. Half a dozen riders, sabres in hands, trotting down the trail. '*Stoi?*' one of them called.

Reilly didn't respond to the challenge. Desperately he tugged at the reins and swung his team to the left. They went over the slight embankment. Behind him the boy called out in alarm. He thought the sledge was going to overturn. But luck was still on Reilly's side. It didn't. The sledge slammed to the ground below and then the horses were off again, manes flying, dodging in and out of the trees in crazy zigzags. Behind him the surprised cavalrymen took up the chase. Their riders slithered down the embankment. Then

262

shouting wildly and waving their sabres above their heads, they came on.

Despite the freezing cold, Reilly felt himself sweating. What was he to do? It wouldn't be long before they caught up with him. His horses numbered three, admittedly, but they were disadvantaged by pulling the heavy sledge.

Frighten them off, a harsh little voice at the back of his mind commanded.

He swung round and fired a shot blindly without aiming. One of the cavalrymen clapped his hand to his shoulder. Next moment he fell heavily from his mount, but the rest kept up the chase.

'Damn you!' he cried, beside himself with rage. 'You won't have me… I'm Sidney Reilly!' Madly he lashed the three horses' glistening rumps with the ends of the reins. They plunged on.

Now one of the riders was trying to outflank him. He came flying in from the right, obviously intent on getting in front of the flying *troika*. Reilly laughed crazily. The cavalryman was just presenting a better target. Again he took the reins in his teeth, Cossack-style. Aiming above the flying manes of his horses, he fired. The cavalryman rose right out of his saddle, propelled upwards by the impact of the slug at such close range and then dropped to the ground, dead before he reached it. His horse turned and began licking his dead master's face, as if it could not understand why he was lying there so silently.

Reilly flashed a look behind him. His pursuers were slowing down. One of them cried something which he couldn't catch above the hiss of the runners. One by one they reined in the mounts. Then they stopped altogether.

Reilly gave a crazy laugh of triumph. He had done it again. *They had given up the chase!*

'Uncle, they have stopped,' the boy said.

He turned and looked at the boy. Now he knew he had to do away with him soon. This had been his last chance. He wouldn't get away with it again. He drove deeper into the forest.

The Lapp and his reindeer were amazing. They moved almost noiselessly through the forest, with the Lapp stopping at periodic intervals to sniff the air. Time and time again he changed direction after doing so, and each time they avoided a new danger by a hair's breath. It was as if their guide could smell danger. In the end Smith concluded that the Lapp's sense of smell was much more highly developed than that of the ordinary city dweller and that he could smell the presence of other men much earlier than they could.

But even with the Lapp's help, Smith felt that they were still in extreme danger. It seemed as if the whole frontier area was alive with troops and police. On all sides there was the light of torches and the clatter of cavalry searching for the fugitives. Once the Lapp dragged them into the snow-heavy bushes at the side of the trail they were on. An instant later a troop of cavalry had jogged by at the trot, their leader flashing his torch to left and right. Smith felt he could have reached out and touched one of them.

Next to him, Mrs Reilly whispered, 'Oh my God, this is becoming too much.'

He could see that even the tough Mrs Reilly was losing hope because of the constant danger. He touched her hand and said, 'It won't be much longer. We'll find them soon – and then we're off.'

Minutes later they were off again, facing a new danger. It was a low-flying aircraft. They couldn't see it in the darkness, but they could hear the steady beat of its engine all right, as it dropped flares above the forest. At regular intervals the flares exploded open with a sharp crack. In an instant the whole area was bathed in an icy white light that revealed everything as the flare slowly dropped to the ground like a fallen angel making the fugitives feel naked and very vulnerable until the damned thing finally was extinguished, leaving them blinking and blinded in the sudden inky darkness.

Still they pushed on, the Lapp guiding them to the appointed rendezvous with that uncanny sense of direction of his, his round Mongol face totally impassive, revealing absolutely no emotion even when lit up by that bright incandescent white light that scared the other three so much.

It was a night of alarms and frights. Once, just as the plane dropped another white flare, a patrol of militiamen surprised them, as the cops emerged suddenly from the snow-heavy bushes. They froze. It was the only thing they could do, with both the Finn and Smith clutching their pistols, hardly daring to breathe. Hearts beating frantically like triphammers, feeling totally naked in the burning white light, they waited for the inevitable. Nothing happened. The militiamen were as blinded by the glare as they

266

were. They staggered past the fugitives, shading their eyes with their free hands and disappeared as abruptly as they had appeared. Their nerve-racking progress continued...

Five miles away, anchored as close to the shore as he dared, Dickie Bird stood on the bridge of the *Swordfish*, worried and nervous, chain-smoking cigarette after cigarette. Next to him, CPO Ferguson puffed morosely at his pipe, saying little, but conveying the feeling that he, too, was just as worried. Time and time again, Dickie glanced at the green-glowing dial of his wristwatch and then peered at the stark black silhouette of the shoreline, as if willing Smith and the rest to appear safely. But the shore remained obstinately empty.

'Can't be much longer now, Chiefie,' he said, perhaps for the third time.

Ferguson took his battered old pipe from his lips and nodded. 'Ay, I'm a-thinking ye're right, Mr Bird. He should nae agone. He only did it for yon woman.' He looked grim.

'Well he has, Chiefie,' Dickie snapped, his usual languid manner vanished. He, too, was tense and nervous. 'But why the devil doesn't he turn up? It'll be first light in a couple of hours' time. Then the cat *will* be among the damned pigeons.'

Across from the mainland came the steady tick-tack of a machine gun. Dickie started and CPO Ferguson looked very worried. He stared through the darkness. But after a few moments the firing stopped and all was silent once more. 'What do you think, Chiefie?' Dickie asked after a moment.

'I dinna know what to think, sir,' Ferguson replied. 'But I think they're in trouble.'

'Exactly my thoughts, Chiefie.'

'But there's nae much we can do about it, sir, ye ken.' Ferguson gave a puff at his old pipe. 'We'll just have to wait on and wee.'

Dickie nodded, but said nothing. He couldn't...

'They're down there somewhere,' Aronson raged. *'Boshe moi!'* he cursed to the pilot of the biplane through the primitive speaking tube which linked the two seats. 'Get down lower!'

'It's dangerous, comrade,' the pilot's dis-embodied voice came back.

'Damn the danger, I want that man,' Aronson snapped. 'Now go lower!'

Reluctantly the pilot agreed.

Below, Reilly heard the plane coming

lower and knew that time had almost run out for him. It was time to abandon the *troika* and then…

Chapter Eight

The Lapp stopped the lead reindeer with a grunted command. Wordlessly he pointed ahead in darkness and said a single word in Finnish.

Smith flashed a look at Finnegan, surprised at the sudden stop. 'Why have we stopped?' he asked. 'What did he say?'

'There,' the little engine driver replied. 'This is it.'

'The rendezvous?' Smith looked at Mrs Reilly, her face set and taut in the cold light of the stars. 'This is where we meet your husband and–'

He broke off. He could hear the hiss of sledge runners and the faint thunder of horses' hooves. He drew his pistol. She did the same. Behind them Finnegan unslung his rifle. Was this Reilly with the boy? Or was it the enemy? They tensed.

Now the sledge came into sight, pulled by

a *troika* of horses.

Finnegan raised his rifle.

'Don't shoot – *yet!*' Smith hissed urgently.

The driver of the *troika* saw them when it was almost too late. Four of them standing in the shadows at the side of the trail, weapons in their hands. For a moment Reilly panicked, almost lost his head. He slewed the sledge round in a great white whirl of snow. Caught by surprise, the boy tumbled out onto the ground. Reilly pulled out his automatic. Desperately he fumbled for the safety catch.

The woman realised immediately what he was going to do. *'No, Sidney… No!'*

'My God!' Smith yelled. 'He's going to kill the boy.' He pressed the trigger of his own weapon. Scarlet flame stabbed the silver darkness. Next to the overturned sledge the bullet struck the trunk of a fir tree, showering Reilly with wood splinters. Abruptly he realised the danger he was in. Crazily, hands trembling with panic, he tugged at the sledge, trying to right it.

'Sidney!' his wife yelled again desperately, as she spotted the boy still lying dazed on the snow. 'Please … please don't!'

He recognized the voice. The veins sticking out at his temples, face scarlet with the effort of trying to right the sledge, he cried, 'You bitch … you treacherous bitch!'

Smith fired again immediately. The slug slammed into the sledge. The horses reared in fear. That did the trick. Suddenly the sledge was upright. Reilly didn't waste any time. He flung himself on to the seat. Frantically he fought to get the crazed horses under control. He knew now he'd make it. He had always done before. He had failed. Yet the next time he wouldn't. He'd work together with the Soviets. They were Red swine, but the secrets he knew of the British Secret Service would save his life. He was sure of that. He lashed the rein ends across the rumps of the horses. They shot forward. Then he was off, the sledge hissing across the snow at a tremendous pace. He turned his head and roared, 'Now they know where you are! Damn your eyes, whoever you are – and you in particular, *whore!*... I hope they kill you slowly...' Then he was gone, disappearing into the silver night in a white wake of flying snow...

The Red cavalry was gaining on them rapidly. The squadron of riders had spread out into two horns, their usual tactic. Now the riders were yelling, their cries savage and exuberant. They knew that the fugitives

271

wouldn't escape now. Before them some-where lay the border river. There they would have to stop. Then they would have the fugitives.

As unperturbed as ever, the Lapp led the two sledges with its new cargo, dodging in and out of the trees as the other three fired the best they could from their violently rocking perches. But their fire was so inaccurate that the cavalrymen weren't even bothering to reply.

Suddenly Smith's nostrils were assailed by a powerful smell of sea salt. 'God,' he cried to the woman, 'there's a marsh out! The river must be a tidal river, flooded by the tide!'

'What?' she gasped. 'What does it mean?'

Smith's heart leapt. 'I think there is a salt marsh up there on this side of the river.' He squeezed the trigger and fired once more. 'The Lapp's taking us to it. Once we hit it, into the reeds with the boy and Finnegan. I think we've got a chance after–'

The sledge lurched. Ahead the reindeer went up to its hocks in frozen muddy water. They had hit the salt marsh. A moment later the second sledge slewed round crazily. Finnegan cursed. His reindeer was up to its knees in the mud, bellowing furiously in a sudden panic, as it found itself trapped.

As the clatter of hooves came ever closer, Smith didn't hesitate. 'Off you go!' he yelled. 'Finnegan, over here!'

Mrs Reilly hesitated and the suddenly terrified boy hesitated. *'Go with the Lapp!'* Smith snarled at the top of his voice.

As the two reindeer, struggling and bellowing in crazy fear, started to sink even deeper, trapped by the heavy sledges they had been pulling, the three of them started through the reeds. Smith watched for a moment, then swung round to face the riders. Out of his pocket he pulled the single grenade he had been saving for just such an emergency. Fingers trembling violently he pulled out the pin, keeping a tight grip on the lever.

Now the riders, clearly visible in the silver light, were only yards away, bending low over the flying manes of their horses, sabres held along their mounts' necks ready for the final kill, wild animal cries coming from their gaping mouths. There were fifteen to twenty of them strung out in a line, slowing down now as they hit the water, their horses' hooves splashing and stumbling in the slippery mud. Smith took a deep breath and said a silent prayer. He let go of the

lever. It pinged off into the water. *'One …
two…'* He counted off the seconds before
the little Mills bomb would explode. *'Three
… four!'* In that same instant, he flung the
grenade and ducked rapidly.

In a vicious spurt of angry yellow and red
flame, the grenade exploded. Vicious, razor-
sharp splinters of metal hissed through the
air on all sides. The riders were caught
completely off guard. In that deadly flame
he could glimpse briefly that terrible scene
of murder and mayhem: horses prancing
wildly, whinnying in agony, blood streaming
down their flanks, men cursing, shouting,
falling, trying to save themselves before
their mounts rolled on them … a rider being
dragged through the mud by his panic-
stricken horse, his head bouncing lifelessly
every time it hit an obstacle. Then all was
darkness once more and he and Finnegan
were on their feet plunging and wading
through the salt mud…

It seemed an age before the Russian
cavalry caught up with them again. Smith,
bringing up the rear, could hear the noisy
splashing and wallowing behind him. To his
front the others were struggling on the best
they could and he knew they were approaching the fiord. The wind brought with it that

old familiar scent of the sea. 'Keep moving!' he yelled desperately. 'We're going to make it. Keep moving!'

He stumbled on, hearing the first rider coming ever closer. Even as he splashed through the icy mud and water, he knew he'd have to do something. The Russians had clearly crossed into Finnish territory and they wouldn't worry about violating it further. He turned and fired. The horse of the first rider reared up into the air, its hooves flailing in an ecstasy of pain. A moment later the injured beast keeled over and flopped into the water with a great splash. But even as the horse fell, its rider swung expertly from his saddle and came after Bird, pistol in hand.

Desperately Smith pressed his trigger once more. Nothing happened! He had run out of ammunition! He cursed with rage and started hurrying after the others. The cavalry-man followed him doggedly, gaining on him all the while.

'The fiord!' Finnegan yelled perhaps some two hundred yards in front. 'And there–'

Smith didn't hear the rest of his words, as the Russian opened fire with his automatic. Scarlet flame stabbed the darkness. Slugs cut the air all around a desperate Smith. He summoned up his last reserves of energy. They were almost there. He had to reach the fiord.

Suddenly the Russian was on him. He could smell that odour of unwashed body, garlic and coarse black tobacco. He turned and brought down his hand in a hard chop. It was an instinctive reaction. It caught the man's wrist. He yelped with pain and dropped his pistol into the muddy water. Smith didn't give him a chance to grab it again. He smashed his clenched fist into the Russian's bearded face. He staggered, yelled something in his own language, but didn't go down. Instead he recovered and his big hands reached out and fastened round Smith's throat in a vicelike grip.

Somewhere there was the roar of engines. Smith had no time for them. Choking and gasping for breath wildly, as the other man's fingers dug cruelly into his throat, he smashed blow after blow into the Russian's bearded face. The cavalryman groaned with pain. Blood flowed thick and hot from his broken nose. Still he did not relax his grip.

Smith was desperate. He was choking to death. Red stars exploded before his eyes. He knew he was losing consciousness. Some instinct for survival told him to search the

Russian's belt. Yes, there it was. A *knife*. With a red veil before his eyes now, threatening to overcome him, he tugged out the blade.

Too late, the Russian realised what the other man was going to do. He released his grip. Smith sucked in a great gulp of life-saving air. Next instant Smith rammed the knife right into the Russian's guts. He screamed shrilly, high and hysterical like a woman. His spine arched like a taut bow-string. Horrified at what he had done, Smith released his hold on the weapon. The Russian's hands flew to the knife, buried up to the hilt in his stomach. Feebly, low moans coming from his suddenly slack lips, he tried to pluck it out. To no avail. He pitched forward slowly. Caught off guard, Smith fell with him. For what seemed an eternity, Smith lay gasping there in the salt marsh, knowing he would never forget this horrific moment for the rest of his life: the man's bearded face, that killing grip, the way the Russian's spine had arched in his death throes. Then the splash and clatter of more Red cavalry alerted him to his dangerous position. He wriggled out from beneath the dead man. Sobbing for breath, the energy draining out of him, as if some invisible trap had been opened, he staggered on, while just off shore, Ginger Kerrigan opened up with his Lewis gun sending warning bursts of tracer zipping into the night…

Now the *Swordfish* was going all out, with the soviets firing everything they had at the frail little wooden craft and Ginger, from his firing position behind the bridge, hosing the shore with slugs in an angry fury of fire.

In the wardroom, the exhausted survivors lay slumped in the battered leather armchairs, sobbing for breath or drinking the scalding hot tea, laced with rum. 'Get some of Nelson's blood down yer, sir,' Billy Bennett had said anxiously, staring at the bedraggled, mud-stained, soaked skipper of the *Swordfish*. 'That'll put new life into yer. Don't worry about that lot on the shore. Couldn't hit a barn door. We'll take care of the sods, if you'll pardon my French, sir.'

Now, as the *Swordfish* started to draw away at a fast lick, sharp prow rising steeply, as the little craft gathered speed by the second, Smith started to rouse himself. Bennett was right. 'Nelson's blood' was doing the trick as it always did. He felt a sense of pleasant warmth steal through his chilled bones.

On the bridge, Dickie Bird, happy now that Smith was back safely, watched the shoreline vanish rapidly into the darkness as he steered the *Swordfish* towards the middle channel of the fiord. Already the enemy fire was beginning to slacken, as the Russians realised that the English had escaped their trap. 'Good by-ee,' he chortled merrily, 'don't cry-ee...' He waved his hand as if in a friendly farewell, and told himself that it was back to jolly old England now and all those jolly old flappers in Mayfair with their short frocks and even lower morals.

Up above, watching the wild wake of the departing *Swordfish*, an enraged Aronson snapped through the speaking tube, 'Pilot get on to the sub with your morse key. Tell Comrade Captain Chekhov that he mustn't fail. He must sink those damned Englishmen at dawn. Or else...'

Chapter Nine

Daylight came late over the Gulf of Finland. It was almost eight before the pale yellow ball of the winter sun rolled over the horizon. It lay there, as if exhausted and unable to go any further, casting no warmth on the bleak winter landscape below. There was snow in the air, Smith could feel it. When it came it would provide the cover they needed, for they were still terribly close to Russia and he already knew that the Soviets were no respecters of other nations' territory. 'Keep a weather eye peeled, Dickie,' he commanded, as he sipped yet another cup of scalding hot tea.

'Like the proverbial tinned tomato, Smithie, old bean,' Dickie Bird answered in his normal chirpy manner. For now they were almost at the exit to the fiord. Soon they'd be out in the Gulf of Finland and on their way home. They'd see Russia no more and for that he was glad. As he had remarked to Smith a little before, 'I've seen the new paradise – Russia – and it don't work, whatever the parlour pinks back home say.'

'Amen to that, Dickie,' Smith had responded heartily. 'Bloody amen to that.'

At eight-thirty, Smith went below, checked that Mrs Reilly and the boy who was apparently fascinated by the first boat he had ever been on in his young life, were all right, poured Finnegan another pink gin – he had been drinking pink gins ever since they had been rescued and still he seemed as sober as a judge – and then ordered the full crew on duty. He posted double watches, went over to Ginger, huddled in a thick sheepskin behind his Lewis gun, and ensured that he had sufficient pans of ammunition at the ready – just in case – and then clattered back up to the bridge where Dickie Bird and CPO Ferguson were steering the *Swordfish* expertly to the narrows which led to the open sea beyond.

He watched the approach in silence for a few moments. It couldn't have been more than five hundred yards across – an ideal place to ambush an enemy. But there wasn't a ship in sight, enemy or otherwise. The grey-green sea was as still as a pond and totally empty. They could have been the last humans alive in the grey-yellow winter world. 'Looks all right to me, Dickie,' he broke the heavy, brooding silence, the only sound the steady throb of the engines. 'What do you think?'

'Safe as houses,' Dickie said cheerfully.

CPO Ferguson wasn't convinced. 'I dinna trust yon foreigners,' he growled in that dour Scottish fashion of his. 'They'd stab ye in the back as soon as they'd look at ye,' he added somewhat obscurely.

Dickie Bird laughed, still happy at the

thought that they were heading for home. 'I don't know, Chiefie,' he said, 'you are a little ray of sunshine, I must–' He stopped short. The smile vanished from his face in a flash. 'What's that?' he snapped.

'What's what?' Smith demanded.

'Over there – to port.'

Smith swung up his glasses and swept the area Dickie was indicating. What looked like a black stove pipe moved silently into the circles of calibrated glass. Behind it there was a faint white wash.

Dickie Bird who had also flung up his glasses at the same time as Smith, rapped, 'Are you thinking what I'm thinking, old bean?'

'I am,' Smith answered grimly. 'A sub.' He stepped across to the alarm and pressed the button. The klaxon burst into noisy, ear-splitting life. Sailors started to tumble out from below, running madly for their duty stations, dragging on extra clothing as they ran.

CPO Ferguson tensed at the wheel as Dickie thrust both throttles forward. He had reacted instinctively. It was going to be highly dangerous, going through the narrows at speed – the charts had shown the bottom was uneven; they might just well hit a rock just below the surface – but he was prepared to take that chance.

Behind the bridge, Ginger Kerrigan swung his Lewis gun round. He'd spotted the submarine periscope, too. He tensed, the gun butt tucked well into his right shoulder, waiting for the order to fire. But even as he did so, he knew his weapon was a mere peashooter when compared with the usual sub's six pounder cannon and a dozen or so torpedoes.

'What do you think, Dickie?' Smith asked urgently, as through the glasses he watched the periscope come nearer.

'I might be wrong. But I wouldn't put it past the Russkis to–' The words froze on his lips. A flurry of exploding bubbles had surfaced to the front of the periscope.

'*Hard to starboard!*' Smith yelled.

CPO Ferguson wrenched the wheel round. In that same instant the first torpedo zipped through the water, trailing bubbles behind, missing the *Swordfish's* wooden bow by feet. Moments later it slammed into the rocky far shore of the narrows and exploded with a great blinding flash of scarlet flame. Shards of rock flew everywhere.

Behind the bridge, Ginger pressed his trigger. He'd try to knock out the periscope, he told himself. It was the eye of the under-water killer. Tracer zipped through the cold air. Bullets splashed into the water all around that evil steel eye. But a desperate Ginger saw he was not hitting the target. 'Cor ferk a duck!' he yelled angrily at the Lewis gun, as if it were human. 'Hit the frigging thing, won't yer!'

At the wheel CPO Ferguson, his craggy old face suddenly ashen, tensed to make his next move with the wheel. He knew his subs. They always fired their tin fish in 'fans' of two or three. He prayed this particular 'fan' would consist only of two torpedoes. He didn't think he could manoeuvre fast enough if the sub commander fired three.

'There she is!' Smith yelled, as there was another flurry of bubbles agitating the surface of the water. He bit his lip. What order should he give? Their unseen enemy was trying to outthink him, just as he was trying to do with the Russian skipper. *Starboard or port?* What was it going to be. *Or–?* The fate of the *Swordfish* and its crew depended upon the decision he made in the next two seconds. Suddenly he had it. '*Full both!*' he yelled above the chatter of the Lewis gun behind him.

Dickie Bird thrust home both throttles. He

knew what Smith was about. The *Swordfish's* Thorneycroft engines responded, at once, beautifully. They burst into full power. The *Swordfish* leapt forward, her deck tilting at a thirty-degree angle, a sudden wild white wake spurting up at her bows.

Two things happened now. Just as the deadly tin fish, containing one ton of high explosive, hissed lethally through the water behind them, with only feet to spare, Ginger's bullets shattered the glass of the submarine's periscope. Ginger let out a great whoop. 'I've got the sod!' he yelled exuber-antly. 'I've blinded the mucker... *Hurrah!*' On the other side of the fiord, the second torpedo exploded into the rocks. Rock flew everywhere, peppering the sea with great lumps like bombs. Angry white founts of water erupted on both sides of the flying *Swordfish.*

But they were not out of danger yet. To port where they had first spotted that peri-scope, the still waters heaved and surged. There was a sudden burst of noise as diesel motors started up. 'They're surfacing!' Ginger yelled from his perch.

A sucking, heaving noise. A sinister black shape broke the surface of the sea. The conning tower hatch was thrown back. Men started to clamber furiously down the outside conning tower ladder. Ginger poised behind his Lewis gun once more and placed a fresh pan of ammunition on it, just as the first black figure dropped the last few dripping rungs.

A sailor flung up his arms, clawing the air as if climbing the rungs of an invisible ladder. Next moment he plunged over the side. But the rest were doubling across the slippery deck, heading for the cannon on the foredeck.

Ginger hosed the deck with his fire. But already the gun crew were protected by the cannon's shield. Tracer howled off the shield like glowing golfballs as the gun crew swung their weapon round to bear on the fleeing torpedo boat. They were well trained, Smith could see that. Above the roar of the Thorneycrofts, he could hear the shell being rammed home. Next instant the gunlayer fired. The first shell ripped through the air with a great roar like a huge sheet of canvas being torn apart.

It burst just to the front of the *Swordfish's* raised prow, erupting in a great geyser of whirling white water.

'They're ranging in!' CPO Ferguson yelled.

'Give her all you've got,' Smith urged Dickie.

His face glazed with sweat in spite of the cold, Dickie pushed the throttles to their furthest extent, as the submarine's cannon belched smoke and fire once again.

The second shell hit the sea just to their rear. Shrapnel hissed lethally through the air. The *Swordfish's* rigging was shorn through. Wires came tumbling to the shell fragment-littered deck. The little craft heeled violently as if it were going to keel over for good. Her speed started to slacken dramatically. Even without looking, Smith knew instinctively they had been hit, probably by a piece of shell, midships.

'She's not responding!' Dickie yelled frantically in the same instant that Ginger struck lucky at last. As the crippled *Swordfish*, going at a snail's pace now, veered to port, the enemy gun crew swung their cannon round to follow them and fire their last shell which they knew would put an end to the crippled boat. For one moment they were exposed, unprotected by their shield.

Ginger didn't wait for a second invitation. He pressed the trigger of his Lewis gun. The ugly machine gun burst into angry life. Blow after blow thudded against his right

287

shoulder as he squinted through the sights, and a stream of glowing white tracer headed straight for the exposed enemy gun crew.

They didn't stand a chance. That vicious burst of savage fire bowled them over like puppets in the hands of a puppetmaster suddenly gone mad. They jerked and shook, their arms flailing crazily, as they dropped writhing to the wet deck or were slammed over the side. In an instant they were all dead or dying and the gun's barrel had drooped, smoke wisps still emerging from it like some primeval monster about to die.

Now for good measure, Ginger directed his fire at the conning tower. Slugs whined and howled off the steel. Bright silver marks appeared as if by magic. Now none of the Russians dared venture out of the tower, and the water was too shallow for the submariners to use their torpedoes. The Russians gave in. Like an ugly steel whale, the Russian sub started to submerge. She'd had enough.

The crew of the *Swordfish* gave a great cheer. They'd won, against all odds. Wearily Smith slumped against the bulkhead of the bridge, feeling utterly worn out while an angry, fuming CPO Ferguson tried to bring the battered little vessel under control. For the old Scot felt that the *Swordfish* was almost his own property. He loved her, he feared her, he dominated her. 'Come, ye fickle hussy!' he snorted. 'Come round, will ye nae, wench!'

Slowly, very slowly, the *Swordfish* started to answer to the wheel. Like an old, old veteran, weary from having fought too many battles, the *Swordfish* began to limp home.

Chapter Ten

At a steady five knots an hour the *Swordfish* limped towards the Swedish port of Sundsvall, where it had all started in what now seemed another age. Smith wasn't taking any more chances, so he decided they would make it to Sweden before they halted to have repair done to the badly battered *Swordfish*.

They still listed and were taking in water. But the crew had laboured like Trojans, Smith told himself, to pump out the seawater. As Ginger had gasped after a two-hour spell at the hand pump, 'Skipper, I'm proper knackered!'

Everyone had been pressed into helping.

Mrs Reilly and the boy had worked side by side, tearing up rags, pieces of cardboard to plug up the *Swordfish's* many holes and prevent any more water coming in. Once she had straightened up, her face dirty, her blouse soaked in fuel oil so that her ample breasts were pressed against the wet silk as if sculpted and had asked, 'What about the boy, de Vere? What will happen to him when we arrive in England?' She had looked lovingly at the boy who was busy plugging yet another hole with the filling from a kapok lifebelt.

Smith had shrugged, other, more important, things on his mind at this moment. 'I will have no say in that,' he answered. 'Our authorities will take care of him.'

'No more authorities,' she had begun almost angrily. Then she had caught herself in time and stopped the angry outburst. Once more she bent to her work, lifting up her skirt and pulling down her underskirt to reveal those lovely legs of hers momentarily, before using the skirt to plug yet another shrapnel hole.

Now, after an agonizing twenty-four hours, when at times Smith had believed they were not going to make it, land came in sight, with a cluster of houses grouped around the tall pointed steeple which was that of Sundsvall's main church. Smith breathed a sigh of relief and pushed his cap to the back of his head a little wearily. Expert shipwrights would patch up the old *Swordfish* in the Swedish port and with luck, they'd be back in England by the weekend.

For a moment or two, as the *Swordfish* crept ever closer to the port, he allowed his mind to dwell on the events of the recent past. How had they managed it? How had they defied the whole power of the Red menace of Communism and achieved what they had come here to do?

'A penny for them, Smithie?' Dickie asked, his voice as weary as Smith's.

He told his old shipmate. Dickie gave a tired laugh. 'Why? I'll tell you, old chap. It's because we're British. All that red on the map kind of stuff. We've simply got the best people. Old Chiefie, Ginger, Sparks, fat Billy Bennett. No other country makes that kind of chap old sport.'

'Of course, you're right, Dickie,' Smith retorted, feeling new energy surge through his tired body at the knowledge that he belonged to a great country and the greatest empire the world had ever seen – the British Empire. 'With chaps like ours, the old country and the British Empire will survive a thousand years. It makes all the hardships and dangers we have been through worthwhile.'

Dickie Bird beamed at him. 'Nothing can beat us, Smithie,' he said enthusiastically. 'We're unique. Nobody like us. Now come on, let's wrap ourselves around a large pink gin before we hit port. We deserve it.'

'That we do.'

Arm and arm the two of them headed for the battered wardroom.

Two hours later, just after the battered and holed *Swordfish* had tied up in the Swedish port to the gasps and comments of the local onlookers, Mrs Reilly came to the wardroom with the boy. 'I have a request, Mr Smith,' she said with her new-found formality.

'Why yes, Mrs Reilly,' Smith said, rising to his feet and thinking what a splendid figure she had under the ragged, stained clothing. 'What is it?'

'Can you lend me some of those sovereigns of yours? I must get some new clothing for myself and the boy. I couldn't possibly arrive in England looking like this. Finnegan' – she used the crew's name for the little Finnish train driver – 'is being paid off as you know. But he says before he sets off for back home, he'll come with us as an interpreter. He speaks some Swedish.'

'Why, of course, Mrs Reilly,' Smith answered hurriedly. 'Anything you want. You – and the boy – deserve it.' He pulled out the moneybag, still stuffed with those 'Horsemen of St George' which had opened doors all the way through for them and said, 'Help yourself.'

She did so and later Smith realised she was avoiding his eyes all the time – but that was later. Eyes still cast down, she said, 'Well, we'll be going now, de Vere.'

'Of course, of course,' he answered, his mind on the problems of getting *Swordfish* seaworthy for her trip back to Hull. 'We'll see you and the boy a little later. And tell Finnegan once again how much we owe the little fellow. He turned out aces.'

'I will,' she said in a subdued voice.

Later he realised she had given him a covert glance at that moment, with a hint of a sheen in her beautiful dark eyes. Now as she went out and he sat down again to his large pink gin, he was more concerned with the Thorneycroft engines which had been damaged in the attack by the Russian submarine in the fiord, saying to Dickie, 'We don't have the time for a real strip-down. We'll see if we can patch it up...'

On the quay, the boy's little hand clutched in hers, Mrs Reilly looked back at the battle-scarred little boat, tears in her eyes. Of course, anything of a long-standing relationship between herself and de Vere was out of the question. She was too old, too tainted, too tough for the young English officer. But she would have dearly loved to have stayed with him a little longer. But that wasn't to be.

At her side, the last of the Romanovs said, 'When are we going shopping, Auntie?'

'Not just yet,' she answered, her heart going out to the boy. Just as she had, he, too, had been ruined by that strange bitter secret war that had been fought in Russia ever since the Revolution. 'But we're going a long way from here. We shall go in a very big boat. And then we'll come to a new country, where there's always plenty of food and where the sun always shines. There you'll be happy.' She looked down at him, the tears streaming down her pretty cheeks unchecked.

The last of the Romanovs didn't notice the tears. Excitedly he chirped, 'In a big boat ... always food and where the sun always shines.' His little face lit up. 'There I'll be happy ... that is, if you'll stay with me, Auntie.'

She pressed his hand winningly and forced a smile. 'Of course I'll stay with you. For ever.'

Together the shabbily dressed woman and the boy in his homespun peasant clothes started to trudge down the winter street, heading for exile and the unknown...

It was two days later when the *Swordfish* was about to sail for home that Smith received the letter with the Stockholm postmark. Puzzled, he opened it and gave a sigh of relief. It was from her. All that day when she had disappeared with the boy, he and the crew of the *Swordfish* had searched the port for her. Again they suspected that Soviet agents might have been at work. It was only when the booking clerk at the station stated that a woman and a boy had bought a ticket – he forgot to where – that Smith had felt a little more at ease. Obviously she had gone of her own volition. To where he couldn't guess. Now as he started to read her note, he realized what her motives had been.

Dearest de Vere, she wrote. *The boy and I have been pawns for others to manipulate for too long. I can't stand the thought that his life should be dominated by the fact that he is 'the last of Romanovs'. He has to have a different future than that. I am going to ensure that he does.*

'I always said the lady was a tough nut with a mind of her own,' Dickie said quietly, as he read the note, too, over Smith's shoulder. Smith nodded and read on.

I shall always treasure the few days we had together. Now I am going a long, long way away where the men who rule our world will never find him. I love you. R.

Smith swallowed hard and put the letter down.

Next to him, Dickie Bird said 'Gosh', but that was all.

It was CPO Ferguson who broke the heavy brooding silence at last. He knocked at the door of the wardroom, came in, cap under his right arm, as if he were back serving on one of His Majesty's battleships, and snapped, *'Swordfish's* ready to sail, sir.'

Smith pulled himself together. 'All right, Chiefie. You don't need to be so shipshape and Bristol-fashion. We're not in the Royal Navy now.'

'Someone's got to keep up standards, sir,' Ferguson growled.

'Take her away then.'

They nosed their way out of the fishing port and then once they were out in the open sea, Ferguson opened the throttles. The Thorneycrofts reacted splendidly. With a wild snarl, the *Swordfish's* prow lifted out of the water. Its speed increased in a flash. The shoreline began to disappear rapidly. Within minutes the *Swordfish* became a mere speck on the hard blue surface of the Baltic. They were going home again.

Common Smith VC, Dickie Bird and all the rest of the crew of the *Swordfish* had written yet another chapter in the secret history of the British Empire...

ENVOI

The Atlanta Journal/
The Atlanta Constitution
Sunday October 9, 1994
From Staff and news services

Serge Reilly, prominent local businessman
and benefactor, has died. Mr Reilly came to
this country it is believed in the '20s, and
opened his own business ten years later. By
the mid-30s he was already a millionaire and
it was then he volunteered to become a
'dollar-a-day' man under the terms of President Roosevelt's 'New Deal'. In 1942,
however, although he was nearly 40, he
volunteered for America's hush-hush OSS
and as a fluent Russian speaker was dropped
by parachute into wartorn Jugoslavia to
assist Marshal Tito's partisans. Subsequently
he was awarded the DSC and the Silver Star.

In later years after the War he gave a great
deal of his wealth away to charities, in particular to the 'New York Society for Aid to
the Victims of Soviet Oppression'. His
widow Mary-Jo Reilly said that this particular charity became almost an obsession

with him. 'He'd have given those Russians the shirt off his back,' she is quoted as saying.

It is perhaps this obsession with matters Russian that explains Mr Reilly's somewhat strange behaviour in the closing years of his life. When he learned of the death of Anastasia Monahan, who had long claimed to be the last surviving member of the Russian Imperial family, though recent DNA tests carried out in England show that she couldn't have been the daughter of the Tsar, Serge Reilly took out paid advertisements in this and other journals proclaiming that he was 'the last of the Romanovs'. Just before his death he wrote an open letter to President Bill Clinton, stating that if the President would help to elevate him to the throne of the new Russia, he would ensure that that country would live 'in peace and prosperity' for all time. President Clinton declined to reply.

Serge Reilly is survived by his widow, Mary-Jo Reilly (née Aronson) and two sons, de Vere and 'Dickie' Reilly. He will be buried in...

This Large Print Book, for people
who cannot read normal print,
is published under the auspices of

THE ULVERSCROFT FOUNDATION

	6	7	8	9	10
			8	19	20